HARRAP'S

Five Adventures of Sherlock Holmes

ARTHUR CONAN DOYLE

A Scandal in Bohemia
First published in *The Strand* in July 1891.

The Five Orange Pips
First published in *The Strand* in November 1891.

Silver Blaze
First published in *The Strand* in December 1892.

The Resident Patient
First published in *The Strand* in August 1893.

The Naval Treaty
First published in *The Strand* in October-November 1893.

21, rue du Montparnasse
75283 Paris CEDEX 06

HARRAP's® est une marque de Larousse SAS
www.harrap.com

ISBN 978 2 81 870886 6

About the author

Arthur Conan Doyle (1859-1930) was born in Edinburgh and studied medicine at the university there. He had an active career as a doctor and ophthalmologist, including volunteering in Bloemfontein during the Boer War[1] and the First World War. But he also wrote historical works and political pamphlets.

Yet it was for his brilliant creation (*A Study in Scarlet*[2], 1881) of the first scientific detective, Sherlock Holmes, that he achieved great fame[3] – so great that after he killed Holmes off to concentrate on his historical work, he was forced to bring the character[4] back to life in *The Hound of the Baskervilles*. In later years, Conan Doyle converted to spiritualism and was a friend of the magician Houdini[5]. He died of a heart attack in 1930, at the age of seventy-one.

1. [en Afrique du Sud, 1899-1902]
2. *Une Étude en rouge*
3. connut une grande célébrité
4. personnage
5. [illusionniste américain]

Direction de la publication : Carine Girac-Marinier

Notes en marge : Etienne Leyris

Révision des notes : Marianne Mouchot

Relecture : F. Le Dantec

Informatique éditoriale et Mise en pages : Philippe Cazabet, Marie-Noëlle Tilliette

Conception graphique : Uli Meindl

Fabrication : Rebecca Dubois

Mot de l'Éditeur

Vous aimeriez lire en langue originale, mais le vocabulaire, les expressions figurées ou la syntaxe vous arrêtent parfois ?

Cette collection est faite pour vous !

Vous trouverez en effet, en note dans la marge, une traduction de certains mots et expressions qui vous permettra d'avancer facilement dans votre lecture.

Nous n'avons pas cherché à vous donner une traduction littéraire de l'ouvrage et nous nous sommes parfois écartés du sens littéral pour vous fournir le sens qui convient le mieux à l'histoire. Aussi les mots sont-ils traduits dans le contexte du texte original.

Les expressions figées anglaises sont, bien entendu, rendues par une expression équivalente en français.

Les allusions à des réalités culturelles du monde anglo-saxon sont expliquées également dans la marge, pour vous aider à mieux comprendre la trame de l'histoire.

Vous aurez ainsi, en regard du texte original, tout le savoir-faire d'un dictionnaire rien que pour vous et adapté à ce livre !

Notre objectif est de vous mener jusqu'au mot FIN en vous donnant les clés nécessaires à la compréhension du récit.

Laissez-vous gagner par l'angoisse, l'humour et le suspense qui règnent chez les maîtres de la littérature anglo-saxonne.

Lire en VO ? You can indeed!

Sommaire

A Scandal in Bohemia 7

The Five Orange Pips 39

Silver Blaze 67

The Resident Patient 103

The Naval Treaty 127

A Scandal in Bohemia

L'énigme que doit résoudre Sherlock Holmes consiste simplement à mettre la main sur une photo compromettante. L'honneur du roi de Bohême est en jeu.

To Sherlock Holmes she is always *the* woman[1]. I have seldom[2] heard him mention her under any other name. In his eyes she eclipses and predominates the whole of her sex. It was not that he felt any emotion akin to[3] love for Irene Adler. All emotions, and that one particularly, were abhorrent to[4] his cold, precise, but admirably balanced[5] mind. He was, I take it[6], the most perfect reasoning and observing machine that the world has seen: but, as a lover, he would have placed himself in a false position. He never spoke of the softer passions, save with a gibe and a sneer[7]. They were admirable things for the observer – excellent for drawing the veil from[8] men's motives[9] and actions. But for the trained[10] reasoner[11] to admit such intrusions into his own delicate and finely adjusted[12] temperament was to introduce a distracting[13] factor which might throw a doubt upon all his mental results. Grit[14] in a sensitive instrument, or a crack[15] in one of his own high-power lenses[16], would not be more disturbing than a strong emotion in a nature such as his. And yet there was but one woman to him[17], and that woman was the late[18] Irene Adler, of dubious and questionable[19] memory.

I had seen little of Holmes lately[20]. My marriage had drifted us away[21] from each other. My own complete happiness, and the home-centred[22] interests which rise up around the man who first[23] finds himself master of his own establishment[24], were sufficient to absorb all my attention; while Holmes, who loathed[25] every form of society[26] with his whole Bohemian soul[27], remained in our lodgings[28] in Baker Street, buried among his old books, and alternating from week to week between

1. *la* femme
2. rarement
3. qui s'apparentât à
4. répugnaient à
5. équilibré
6. je suppose
7. sauf pour les railler
8. lever le voile sur
9. les mobiles
10. aguerri
11. logicien
12. réglé
13. perturbateur
14. Un grain de sable
15. fêlure
16. loupes de haute précision
17. il n'y avait qu'une seule femme à ses yeux
18. feu
19. très douteuse
20. ces derniers temps
21. nous avait éloignés
22. domestiques
23. pour la première fois
24. foyer
25. détestait
26. vie sociale
27. de toute sa nature bohème
28. meublé

cocaine and ambition, the drowsiness of[1] the drug, and the fierce[2] energy of his own keen[3] nature. He was still, as ever, deeply attracted by the study of crime, and occupied his immense faculties and extraordinary powers of observation in following out those clues[4], and clearing up[5] those mysteries, which had been abandoned as hopeless by the official police. From time to time I heard some vague account[6] of his doings[7]: of his summons[8] to Odessa in the case of the Trepoff murder, of his clearing up of[9] the singular tragedy of the Atkinson brothers at Trincomalee, and finally of the mission which he had accomplished so delicately[10] and successfully for the reigning family of Holland. Beyond these signs of his activity, however, which I merely[11] shared with all the readers of the daily press, I knew little of my former[12] friend and companion.

One night – it was on the 20th of March, 1888 – I was returning from a journey to a patient[13] (for[14] I had now returned to civil practice[15]), when my way led me through Baker Street. As I passed the well remembered door, which must always be associated in my mind with my wooing[16], and with the dark incidents of the *Study in Scarlet*, I was seized with a keen[17] desire to see Holmes again, and to know how he was employing his extraordinary powers. His rooms were brilliantly lit, and, even as[18] I looked up, I saw his tall spare figure[19] pass twice in a dark silhouette against the blind[20]. He was pacing[21] the room swiftly, eagerly[22], with his head sunk upon his chest, and his hands clasped behind him[23]. To me, who knew his every mood and habit[24], his attitude and manner told their own story[25]. He was at work again. He had risen out of his drug-created dreams, and was hot upon the scent[26] of some new problem. I rang the bell, and

1. léthargie induite par
2. farouche
3. intense
4. à remonter les pistes
5. à élucider
6. récit
7. activités
8. qu'on l'avait appelé
9. qu'il avait élucidé
10. avec tant de tact
11. simplement
12. ancien
13. visite chez un patient
14. car
15. j'exerçais à nouveau dans le civil
16. la période où je faisais ma cour
17. vif
18. au moment même où
19. haute et mince silhouette
20. sur le store
21. arpentait
22. d'un pas vif et ardent
23. les mains dans le dos
24. la moindre de ses humeurs et de ses habitudes
25. parlaient d'elles-mêmes
26. était sur la piste

was shown up[1] to the chamber which had formerly[2] been in part my own.

His manner was not effusive[3]. It seldom was; but he was glad, I think, to see me. With hardly a word spoken, but with a kindly[4] eye, he waved me to[5] an armchair, threw across his case of cigars, and indicated a spirit case[6] and a gasogene[7] in the corner. Then he stood before the fire, and looked me over in his singular introspective fashion.

'Wedlock suits you[8],' he remarked. 'I think, Watson, that you have put on[9] seven and a half pounds since I saw you.'

'Seven,' I answered.

'Indeed, I should have thought a little more. Just a trifle more[10], I fancy[11], Watson. And in practice again[12], I observe. You did not tell me that you intended to go into harness[13].'

'Then, how do you know?'

'I see it, I deduce it. How do I know that you have been getting yourself very wet lately, and that you have a most clumsy[14] and careless[15] servant girl?'

'My dear Holmes,' said I, 'this is too much. You would certainly have been burned had you lived[16] a few centuries ago. It is true that I had a country walk on Thursday and came home in a dreadful mess[17]; but, as I have changed my clothes, I can't imagine how you deduce it. As to Mary Jane, she is incorrigible, and my wife has given her notice[18]; but there again I fail to see how you work it out[19].'

He chuckled to himself[20] and rubbed his long nervous hands together.

'It is simplicity itself,' said he; 'my eyes tell me that on the inside of your left shoe, just where the firelight strikes it, the leather is scored[21] by six almost parallel cuts[22]. Obviously they have been caused by some one who has very carelessly scraped round

1. mené
2. auparavant
3. Il ne se montra guère expansif
4. bienveillant
5. du geste il m'indiqua
6. cave à spiritueux
7. siphon d'eau de Seltz
8. Le mariage vous va bien
9. pris
10. un tout petit peu plus
11. dirais-je
12. de nouveau en exercice
13. de reprendre le collier
14. empotée
15. négligente
16. si vous aviez vécu
17. en piteux état
18. l'a congédiée
19. devinez cela
20. rit dans sa barbe
21. éraflé
22. stries

the edges of the sole[1] in order to remove crusted mud from it[2]. Hence[3], you see, my double deduction that you had been out in vile weather[4], and that you had a particularly malignant[5] boot-slitting[6] specimen of the London slavey[7]. As to your practice[8], if a gentleman walks into my rooms smelling of iodoform, with a black mark of nitrate of silver upon his right forefinger, and a bulge[9] on the side of his top hat to show where he has secreted[10] his stethoscope, I must be dull indeed[11] if I do not pronounce him to be an active member of the medical profession.'

I could not help laughing at the ease[12] with which he explained his process of deduction. 'When I hear you give your reasons,' I remarked, 'the thing always appears to me to be so ridiculously simple that I could easily do it myself, though at each successive instance[13] of your reasoning I am baffled[14], until you explain your process. And yet[15] I believe that my eyes are as good as yours.'

'Quite so,' he answered, lighting a cigarette, and throwing himself down into an armchair. 'You see, but you do not observe. The distinction is clear. For example, you have frequently seen the steps which lead up from the hall to this room.'

'Frequently.'

'How often?'

'Well, some hundreds of times.'

'Then how many are there?'

'How many! I don't know.'

'Quite so! You have not observed. And yet you have seen. That is just my point[16]. Now, I know that there are seventeen steps, because I have both seen and observed. By the way[17], since you are interested in these little problems, and since you are good enough to chronicle[18] one or two of my trifling[19] experiences, you may be interested in this.' He

1. frotté les bords de la semelle
2. la boue qui s'y était incrustée
3. D'où
4. par très mauvais temps
5. détestable
6. massacreur de chaussures
7. gent domestique londonienne
8. activité médicale
9. bosse
10. a dissimulé
11. passablement stupide
12. aisance
13. étape
14. perplexe
15. pourtant
16. C'est exactement ce que je veux dire
17. À propos
18. relater
19. insignifiantes

threw over a sheet of thick pink-tinted[1] notepaper[2] which had been lying open upon the table. 'It came by the last post,' said he. 'Read it aloud.'

The note was undated, and without either signature or address.

'There will call upon you[3] tonight, at a quarter to eight o'clock,' it said, 'a gentleman who desires to consult you upon a matter[4] of the very deepest moment[5]. Your recent services to one of the Royal Houses of Europe have shown that you are one who may safely be trusted with[6] matters which are of an importance which can hardly be exaggerated. This account of you[7] we have from all quarters received[8]. Be in your chamber then at that hour, and do not take it amiss[9] if your visitor wear a mask.'

'This is indeed a mystery,' I remarked. 'What do you imagine that it means?'

'I have no data yet. It is a capital mistake[10] to theorise before one has data[11]. Insensibly one[12] begins to twist[13] facts to suit[14] theories, instead of theories to suit facts. But the note itself. What do you deduce from it?'

I carefully examined the writing, and the paper upon which it was written.

'The man who wrote it was presumably well-to-do[15],' I remarked, endeavouring[16] to imitate my companion's processes[17]. 'Such paper could not be bought under half a crown a packet. It is peculiarly strong and stiff[18].'

'Peculiar[19] – that is the very word[20],' said Holmes. 'It is not an English paper at all. Hold it up to the light.'

I did so, and saw a large *E* with a small *g*, a *P*, and a large *G* with a small *t* woven into the texture of the paper[21].

'What do you make of that?' asked Holmes.

1. de couleur rose
2. billet
3. Viendra vous rendre visite
4. au sujet d'une affaire
5. de la plus haute importance
6. quelqu'un à qui l'on peut soumettre en toute confiance
7. Un tel jugement sur vous
8. nous est de toutes parts parvenu
9. ne le prenez pas mal
10. erreur grossière
11. d'avoir des informations
12. on
13. à déformer
14. pour qu'ils collent aux
15. sans doute fortuné
16. m'efforçant
17. la façon de procéder
18. rigide
19. Particulier
20. mot juste
21. en filigrane

'The name of the maker, no doubt; or his monogram, rather.'

'Not at all. The *G* with the small *t* stands for[1] "Gesellschaft," which is the German for "Company." It is a customary[2] contraction[3] like our "Co[4]." *P*, of course, stands for "Papier." Now for[5] the *Eg*. Let us glance at our Continental Gazetteer[6].' He took down a heavy brown volume from his shelves. 'Eglow, Eglonitz – here we are, Egria[7]. It is in a German-speaking country – in Bohemia, not far from Carlsbad. "Remarkable as being the scene of the death of Wallenstein[8], and for its numerous glass factories and paper mills[9]." Ha, ha, my boy, what do you make of that?' His eyes sparkled[10], and he sent up a great blue triumphant cloud from his cigarette.

'The paper was made in Bohemia,' I said.

'Precisely. And the man who wrote the note is a German. Do you note the peculiar construction of the sentence – "This account of you we have from all quarters received." A Frenchman or Russian could not have written that. It is the German who is so uncourteous to[11] his verbs. It only remains, therefore[12], to discover what is wanted by this German who writes upon Bohemian paper, and prefers wearing a mask to showing his face. And here he comes, if I am not mistaken, to resolve[13] all our doubts.'

As he spoke there was the sharp sound of horses' hoofs and grating wheels against the kerb[14], followed by a sharp pull at the bell. Holmes whistled.

'A pair by the sound[15],' said he. 'Yes,' he continued, glancing out of the window. 'A nice little brougham[16] and a pair of beauties[17]. A hundred and fifty guineas apiece[18]. There's money in this case[19], Watson, if there is nothing else[20].'

'I think that I had better go, Holmes.'

1. signifie
2. courante
3. abréviation
4. Cie
5. Et maintenant
6. Annuaire
7. Egra [l'actuelle Cheb, en République tchèque]
8. [général d'origine tchèque (1583-1634), au service de l'empereur pendant la guerre de Trente Ans]
9. fabriques de papier
10. pétillaient
11. discourtois envers
12. par conséquent
13. pour lever
14. de roues râpant la bordure du trottoir
15. à en juger par le bruit
16. coupé
17. deux belles bêtes
18. chacune
19. affaire
20. à défaut d'autre chose

'Not a bit[1], Doctor. Stay where you are. I am lost without my Boswell[2]. And this promises to be interesting. It would be a pity[3] to miss it[4].'

'But your client–'

'Never mind him[5]. I may want your help, and so may he. Here he comes. Sit down in that armchair, Doctor, and give us your best attention.'

A slow and heavy step[6], which had been heard upon the stairs and in the passage, paused immediately outside[7] the door. Then there was a loud and authoritative tap[8].

'Come in!' said Holmes.

A man entered who could hardly have been less than six feet six inches in height[9], with the chest and limbs[10] of a Hercules. His dress was rich with a richness which would, in England, be looked upon as akin to bad taste[11]. Heavy bands of astrakhan were slashed across[12] the sleeves and fronts of his double-breasted coat[13], while the deep blue cloak[14] which was thrown over his shoulders was lined[15] with flame-coloured silk[16], and secured[17] at the neck with a brooch which consisted of a single flaming[18] beryl. Boots which extended half-way up his calves[19], and which were trimmed at the tops with rich[20] brown fur, completed the impression of barbaric opulence which was suggested by his whole appearance. He carried a broad-brimmed[21] hat in his hand, while he wore across the upper part of his face, extending down past the cheekbones, a black vizard[22] mask, which he had apparently adjusted that very moment[23], for his hand was still raised to it as he entered. From the lower part of the face he appeared to be a man of strong character, with a thick, hanging lip, and a long straight chin, suggestive of resolution[24] pushed to the length of obstinacy[25].

1. Pas du tout
2. sans mon biographe et ami [de Samuel Johnson, lexicographe du XVIIIe s.]
3. dommage
4. de manquer l'occasion
5. N'en tenez pas compte
6. pas
7. juste derrière
8. on frappa, avec force et autorité
9. faire moins de 1,98 m
10. les membres
11. jugée de mauvais goût
12. barraient
13. manteau croisé
14. cape
15. doublée
16. soie rouge vif
17. attachée
18. flamboyant
19. lui arrivaient à mi-mollet
20. bordées d'une belle
21. à large bord
22. à visière
23. à l'instant
24. volonté
25. jusqu'à l'obstination

1. dure
2. viendrais vous voir
3. Je vous en prie,

'You had my note?' he asked, with a deep, harsh[1] voice and a strongly marked German accent. 'I told you that I would call[2].' He looked from one to the other of us, as if uncertain which to address.

'Pray[3] take a seat,' said Holmes. 'This is my friend and colleague, Dr. Watson, who is occasionally good enough to help me in my cases. Whom have I the honour to address?'

'You may address me as the Count von Kramm, a Bohemian nobleman. I understand that this gentleman, your friend, is a man of honour and discretion, whom I may trust with a matter of the most extreme importance. If not, I should much prefer to communicate with you alone.'

4. nous deux ou personne
5. haussa
6. par exiger de tous deux
7. sa portée est telle

I rose to go, but Holmes caught me by the wrist and pushed me back into my chair. 'It is both, or none[4],' said he. 'You may say before this gentleman anything which you may say to me.'

The Count shrugged[5] his broad shoulders. 'Then I must begin,' said he, 'by binding you both to[6] absolute secrecy for two years, at the end of that time the matter will be of no importance. At present it is not too much to say that it is of such weight[7] that it may have an influence upon European history.'

'I promise,' said Holmes.

'And I.'

'You will excuse this mask,' continued our strange visitor. 'The august person who employs me wishes his agent to be unknown to you, and I may confess at once that the title by which I have just called myself is not exactly my own.'

8. m'en étais rendu compte
9. sèchement
10. étouffer

'I was aware of it[8],' said Holmes dryly[9].

'The circumstances are of great delicacy, and every precaution has to be taken to quench[10] what might grow to be an immense scandal and seriously compromise one of the reigning families of Europe.

To speak plainly[1], the matter implicates the great House of Ormstein, hereditary kings of Bohemia.'

'I was also aware of that,' murmured Holmes, settling himself down[2] in his armchair, and closing his eyes.

Our visitor glanced with some apparent surprise at the languid[3], lounging[4] figure[5] of the man who had been no doubt depicted to him[6] as the most incisive reasoner, and most energetic agent in Europe. Holmes slowly reopened his eyes, and looked impatiently at his gigantic client.

'If your Majesty would condescend to state your case[7],' he remarked, 'I should be better able to advise you[8].'

The man sprang from his chair, and paced up and down[9] the room in uncontrollable agitation. Then, with a gesture of desperation, he tore the mask from his face and hurled it[10] upon the ground. 'You are right,' he cried, 'I am the King. Why should I attempt to conceal it?'

'Why, indeed?' murmured Holmes. 'Your Majesty had not spoken before I was aware that I was addressing[11] Wilhelm Gottsreich Sigismond von Ormstein, Grand Duke of Cassel-Falstein, and hereditary King of Bohemia.'

'But you can understand,' said our strange visitor, sitting down once more and passing his hand over his high, white forehead, 'you can understand that I am not accustomed to doing such business in my own person. Yet the matter was so delicate that I could not confide it[12] to an agent without putting myself in his power. I have come incognito from Prague for the purpose[13] of consulting you.'

'Then, pray consult,' said Holmes, shutting his eyes once more.

1. sans détour
2. en se calant
3. indolente
4. abandonnée
5. silhouette
6. lui avait sans doute été dépeint
7. exposer son affaire
8. de la conseiller
9. se mit à arpenter
10. le lança
11. que je me savais déjà en face de
12. la confier
13. dans le but

'The facts are briefly these: Some five years ago, during a lengthy[1] visit to Warsaw[2], I made the acquaintance[3] of the well-known adventuress[4] Irene Adler. The name is no doubt familiar to you.'

'Kindly[5] look her up[6] in my index, Doctor,' murmured Holmes, without opening his eyes. For many years he had adopted a system of docketing[7] all paragraphs[8] concerning men and things, so that it was difficult to name a subject or a person on which he could not at once furnish information. In this case I found her biography sandwiched in between[9] that of a Hebrew Rabbi[10] and that of a staff-commander[11] who had written a monograph upon the deep-sea fishes.

'Let me see,' said Holmes. 'Hum! Born in New Jersey in the year 1858. Contralto – hum! La Scala, hum! Prima donna Imperial Opera of Warsaw – Yes! Retired from operatic stage[12] – ha! Living in London – quite so! Your Majesty, as I understand, became entangled[13] with this young person, wrote her some compromising letters, and is now desirous of getting those letters back.'

'Precisely so. But how–'

'Was there a secret marriage?'

'None.'

'No legal papers or certificates?'

'None.'

'Then I fail to follow[14] Your Majesty. If this young person should produce her letters for blackmailing[15] or other purposes, how is she to prove their authenticity?'

'There is the writing.'

'Pooh[16], pooh! Forgery[17].'

'My private notepaper[18].'

'Stolen.'

'My own seal[19].'

1. longue
2. Varsovie
3. connaissance
4. aventurière
5. Ayez l'obligeance de
6. chercher son nom
7. catalogage
8. de toutes les brèves
9. coincée entre
10. rabbin
11. commandant en second
12. la scène lyrique
13. a eu une aventure
14. ne suis pas très bien
15. exercer un chantage
16. Peuh
17. Une contrefaçon
18. papier à lettres personnel
19. cachet

'Imitated.'

'My photograph.'

'Bought.'

'We were both in[1] the photograph.'

'Oh, dear! That is very bad! Your Majesty has indeed committed an indiscretion[2].'

'I was mad – insane[3].'

'You have compromised yourself seriously.'

'I was only Crown Prince[4] then. I was young. I am but thirty[5] now.'

'It must be recovered[6].'

'We have tried and failed[7].'

'Your Majesty must pay. It must be bought.'

'She will not sell.'

'Stolen, then.'

'Five attempts[8] have been made. Twice burglars[9] in my pay[10] ransacked her house[11]. Once we diverted[12] her luggage when she travelled. Twice she has been waylaid[13]. There has been no result.'

'No sign of it?'

'Absolutely none.'

Holmes laughed. 'It is quite a pretty little problem,' said he.

'But a very serious one to me,' returned the King, reproachfully.

'Very, indeed. And what does she propose to do with the photograph?'

'To ruin me.'

'But how?'

'I am about to be married[14].'

'So I have heard[15].'

'To Clotilde Lothman von Saxe-Meningen, second daughter of the King of Scandinavia. You may know the strict principles of her family. She is herself the very soul of delicacy[16]. A shadow of

1. sur
2. imprudence
3. toqué
4. prince héritier
5. n'ai que 30 ans
6. Il faut la récupérer
7. échoué
8. tentatives
9. des cambrioleurs
10. à ma solde
11. ont mis sa maison sens dessus dessous
12. avons détourné
13. prise en embuscade
14. sur le point de me marier
15. Il paraît
16. la délicatesse personnifiée

a doubt as to[1] my conduct would bring the matter to an end[2].'

'And Irene Adler?'

'Threatens[3] to send them the photograph. And she will do it. I know that she will do it. You do not know her, but she has a soul of steel[4]. She has the face of the most beautiful of women, and the mind of the most resolute of men. Rather than I should[5] marry another woman, there are no lengths to which she would not go[6] – none[7].'

'You are sure that she has not sent it yet?'

'I am sure.'

'And why?'

'Because she has said that she would send it on the day when the betrothal[8] was publicly proclaimed. That will be next Monday.'

'Oh, then, we have three days yet,' said Holmes, with a yawn[9]. 'That is very fortunate[10], as I have one or two matters of importance to look into[11] just at present. Your Majesty will, of course, stay in London for the present?'

'Certainly. You will find me at the Langham, under the name of the Count von Kramm.'

'Then I shall drop you a line[12] to let you know how we progress.'

'Pray do so. I shall be all anxiety.'

'Then, as to money?'

'You have *carte blanche*.'

'Absolutely?'

'I tell you that I would give one of the provinces of my kingdom to have that photograph.'

'And for present expenses[13]?'

The King took a heavy chamois leather bag from under his cloak, and laid it on the table.

'There are three hundred pounds in gold, and seven hundred in notes[14],' he said.

1. concernant
2. mettrait un terme à nos projets
3. Elle menace
4. âme inflexible
5. Plutôt que de me voir
6. elle serait prête à toutes les extrémités
7. toutes
8. les fiançailles
9. bâillement
10. heureux
11. à examiner
12. vous enverrai un mot
13. les frais immédiats
14. en billets

Holmes scribbled[1] a receipt[2] upon a sheet of his notebook, and handed it to him.

'And mademoiselle's address?' he asked.

'Is Briony Lodge, Serpentine Avenue, St. John's Wood.'

Holmes took a note of it. 'One other question,' said he. 'Was the photograph a cabinet[3]?'

'It was.'

'Then, good night, Your Majesty, and I trust[4] that we shall soon have some good news for you. And good night, Watson,' he added, as the wheels of the Royal brougham rolled down the street. 'If you will be good enough to call[5] tomorrow afternoon, at three o'clock, I should like to chat this little matter over with you[6].'

At three o'clock precisely I was at Baker Street, but Holmes had not yet returned. The landlady[7] informed me that he had left the house shortly after eight o'clock in the morning. I sat down beside the fire, however, with the intention of awaiting him, however long he might be[8]. I was already deeply interested in his inquiry, for, though it was surrounded by none of the grim[9] and strange features[10] which were associated with the two crimes which I have elsewhere recorded[11], still, the nature of the case and the exalted station[12] of his client gave it a character of its own[13]. Indeed, apart from the nature of the investigation which my friend had on hand[14], there was something in his masterly[15] grasp[16] of a situation, and his keen[17], incisive reasoning, which made it a pleasure to me to study his system of work, and to follow the quick, subtle methods by which he disentangled[18] the most inextricable mysteries. So accustomed was I to his

1. griffonna
2. un reçu
3. format album
4. j'ai bon espoir
5. vous présenter
6. causer avec vous de cette petite affaire
7. logeuse
8. aussi longtemps qu'il le faudrait
9. sinistres
10. caractéristiques
11. relatés ailleurs [dans *Une Étude en rouge* et *Le Signe des quatre*]
12. position sociale très élevée
13. cachet particulier
14. en cours
15. magistrale
16. compréhension
17. pénétrant
18. démêlait

invariable success that the very possibility of his failing[1] had ceased to enter into my head.

It was close upon four[2] before the door opened, and a drunken-looking[3] groom[4], ill-kempt[5] and side-whiskered[6], with an inflamed face and disreputable[7] clothes, walked into the room. Accustomed as I was[8] to my friend's amazing powers in the use of disguises[9], I had to look three times before I was certain that it was indeed he. With a nod[10] he vanished into the bedroom, whence[11] he emerged in five minutes tweed-suited[12] and respectable, as of old[13]. Putting his hands into his pockets, he stretched out his legs in front of the fire, and laughed heartily[14] for some minutes.

'Well, really!' he cried, and then he choked[15]; and laughed again until he was obliged to lie back, limp and helpless[16], in the chair.

'What is it?'

'It's quite[17] too funny. I am sure you could never guess how I employed my morning, or what I ended by doing.'

'I can't imagine. I suppose that you have been watching the habits[18], and perhaps the house, of Miss Irene Adler.'

'Quite so, but the sequel[19] was rather unusual. I will tell you, however. I left the house a little after eight o'clock this morning, in the character of a groom out of work[20]. There is a wonderful sympathy and freemasonry[21] among horsey men[22]. Be one of them, and you will know all that there is to know. I soon found Briony Lodge. It is a bijou villa[23], with a garden at the back, but built out in front right up to[24] the road, two stories[25]. Chubb lock[26] to the door. Large sitting-room on the right side, well furnished, with long windows almost to the floor, and those preposterous[27] English window

1. la possibilité même qu'il échouât
2. près de quatre heures
3. semblant pris de boisson
4. garçon d'écurie
5. négligé
6. pourvu de favoris
7. pitoyables
8. Tout familier que je fusse
9. déguisements
10. hochement de tête,
11. d'où
12. en costume de tweed
13. comme avant
14. de bon cœur
15. s'étouffa
16. à bout de forces
17. vraiment
18. habitudes
19. résultat
20. au chômage
21. solidarité
22. entre gens de cheval
23. un bijou de villa
24. jusqu'au bord de
25. niveaux
26. Serrure à gorges
27. ridicules

fasteners[1] which a child could open. Behind there was nothing remarkable, save[2] that the passage window could be reached from the top of the coach-house[3]. I walked round it and examined it closely[4] from every point of view, but without noting anything else of interest.

'I then lounged down[5] the street, and found, as I expected, that there was a mews[6] in a lane[7] which runs down by[8] one wall of the garden. I lent the ostlers a hand[9] in rubbing down[10] their horses, and I received in exchange twopence, a glass of half-and-half[11], two fills of shag tobacco[12] and as much information as I could desire about Miss Adler, to say nothing of[13] half a dozen other people in the neighbourhood[14] in whom I was not in the least interested, but whose biographies I was compelled[15] to listen to.'

'And what of[16] Irene Adler?' I asked.

'Oh, she has turned all the men's heads down in that part[17]. She is the daintiest thing under a bonnet[18] on this planet. So say the Serpentine Mews, to a man[19]. She lives quietly, sings at concerts, drives out at five every day, and returns at seven sharp[20] for dinner. Seldom goes out at other times, except when she sings. Has only one male visitor, but a good deal of him[21]. He is dark, handsome, and dashing[22]; never calls less than[23] once a day, and often twice. He is a Mr. Godfrey Norton, of the Inner Temple[24]. See the advantages of a cabman as a confidant[25]. They had driven him home a dozen times from Serpentine Mews, and knew all about him. When I had listened to all that they had to tell, I began to walk up and down near Briony Lodge once more, and to think over[26] my plan of campaign.

1. fermetures
2. si ce n'est
3. remise à voiture
4. attentivement
5. J'ai ensuite descendu tranquillement
6. des écuries
7. ruelle
8. longe
9. J'ai aidé les valets d'écurie
10. à bouchonner
11. bière [mi-brune mi-blonde]
12. pipes de tabac à rouler
13. sans parler de
14. du voisinage
15. forcé
16. alors,
17. le quartier
18. la plus jolie fille qui soit
19. tous sans exception
20. à sept heures précises
21. qui vient très souvent
22. fringant
23. il vient au moins
24. [l'un des sites londoniens du barreau britannique]
25. d'être le confident d'un cocher
26. à réfléchir à

'This Godfrey Norton was evidently an important factor in the matter. He was a lawyer[1]. That sounded ominous[2]. What was the relation between them, and what the object of his repeated visits? Was she his client, his friend, or his mistress? If the former[3], she had probably transferred the photograph to his keeping[4]. If the latter[5], it was less likely. On the issue of[6] this question depended whether[7] I should continue my work at Briony Lodge, or[8] turn my attention to the gentleman's chambers[9] in the Temple. It was a delicate point, and it widened[10] the field of my inquiry. I fear that I bore you[11] with these details, but I have to let you see my little difficulties, if you are to understand the situation.'

'I am following you closely[12],' I answered.

'I was still balancing the matter in my mind[13] when a hansom cab[14] drove up to Briony Lodge, and a gentleman sprang out. He was a remarkably handsome man, dark, aquiline, and moustached – evidently the man of whom I had heard. He appeared to be in a great hurry, shouted to the cabman to wait, and brushed past the maid[15] who opened the door with the air of a man who was thoroughly at home[16].

'He was in the house about half an hour, and I could catch glimpses of him[17], in the windows of the sitting-room, pacing up and down[18], talking excitedly and waving his arms. Of her I could see nothing. Presently[19] he emerged[20], looking even more flurried[21] than before. As he stepped up to the cab, he pulled a gold watch from his pocket and looked at it earnestly. 'Drive like the devil[22]," he shouted, "first to Gross and Hankey's in Regent Street, and then to the church of St. Monica in the Edgware Road. Half a guinea if you do it in twenty minutes!'

1. avocat
2. de mauvais augure
3. Dans le premier cas
4. lui avait probablement confié la photographie
5. Dans le dernier cas
6. Selon la réponse à
7. soit
8. soit
9. appartement
10. élargissait
11. de vous ennuyer
12. avec attention
13. balançais encore
14. fiacre
15. fila derrière la servante
16. connaissait parfaitement les lieux
17. l'entrevoir
18. marchant de long en large
19. Bientôt
20. ressortit
21. agité
22. à bride abattue

'Away they went, and I was just wondering whether I should not do well to follow them, when up the lane came a neat little landau, the coachman with his coat only half buttoned, and his tie under his ear, while all the tags[1] of his harness were sticking out of the buckles[2]. It hadn't pulled up before she[3] shot out of the hall door[4] and into it[5]. I only caught a glimpse of her[6] at the moment, but she was a lovely woman, with a face that a man might die for.

'"The Church of St. Monica, John," she cried, "and half a sovereign if you reach it in twenty minutes."

'This was quite too good to lose[7], Watson. I was just balancing whether[8] I should run for it[9], or whether I should perch behind her landau, when a cab came through the street. The driver looked twice at such a shabby fare[10]; but I jumped in before he could object. "The Church of St. Monica," said I, "and half a sovereign if you reach it in twenty minutes." It was twenty-five minutes to twelve[11], and of course it was clear enough what was in the wind[12].

'My cabby[13] drove fast. I don't think I ever drove faster, but the others were there before us. The cab and the landau with their steaming[14] horses were in front of the door when I arrived. I paid the man and hurried into the church. There was not a soul there save[15] the two whom I had followed, and a surpliced[16] clergyman, who seemed to be expostulating[17] with them. They were all three standing in a knot[18] in front of the altar[19]. I lounged up[20] the side aisle[21] like any other idler[22] who has dropped into a church. Suddenly, to my surprise, the three at the altar faced round to me, and Godfrey Norton came running as hard as he could towards me.

'"Thank God!" he cried. "You'll do[23]. Come! Come!"

1. courroies
2. n'étaient qu'à moitié attachées
3. L'attelage n'avait pas fait halte qu'elle
4. franchissait la porte d'entrée en trombe
5. sautait dans la voiture
6. n'ai fait que l'entrapercevoir
7. L'occasion était trop belle
8. hésitais à
9. m'y rendre en courant
10. ce client aussi mal fagotté
11. [heure limite pour la célébration d'un mariage]
12. ce qui se tramait était très clair
13. cocher
14. tout fumants
15. sauf
16. en surplis
17. discuter très vivement
18. regroupés
19. autel
20. ai remonté tranquillement
21. bas-côté
22. flâneur
23. ferez l'affaire

'"What then[1]?" I asked.

'"Come, man, come, only three minutes, or it won't be legal."

'I was half dragged up to[2] the altar, and before I knew where I was, I found myself mumbling[3] responses which were whispered in my ear, and vouching for[4] things of which I knew nothing, and generally assisting in the secure tying up[5] of Irene Adler, spinster[6], to Godfrey Norton, bachelor[7]. It was all done in an instant, and there was the gentleman thanking me on the one side and the lady on the other, while the clergyman beamed on me[8] in front. It was the most preposterous position in which I ever found myself in my life, and it was the thought of it that started me laughing just now. It seems that there had been some informality about their licence[9], that the clergyman absolutely refused to marry them without a witness[10] of some sort, and that my lucky[11] appearance[12] saved the bridegroom[13] from having to sally out into the streets in search[14] of a best man[15]. The bride gave me a sovereign, and I mean to[16] wear it on my watch-chain in memory of the occasion.'

'This is a very unexpected turn of affairs[17],' said I; 'and what then?'

'Well, I found my plans very seriously menaced[18]. It looked as if the pair[19] might take an immediate departure, and so necessitate very prompt and energetic measures on my part. At the church door, however, they separated, he driving back to the Temple, and she to her own house. "I shall drive out in the Park at five as usual," she said as she left him. I heard no more. They drove away in different directions, and I went off to make my own arrangements[20].'

'Which are?'

1. Que se passe-t-il
2. On m'a entraîné jusqu'à
3. à bredouiller
4. répondant de
5. union
6. demoiselle
7. célibataire
8. me regardait, rayonnant
9. irrégularité s'opposait à leur union
10. témoin
11. providentielle
12. survenue
13. a évité au fiancé
14. de devoir sortir à la recherche
15. garçon d'honneur
16. je compte
17. L'affaire a pris un tour très inattendu
18. compromis
19. le couple
20. dispositions

'Some cold beef and a glass of beer,' he answered, ringing the bell. 'I have been too busy to think of food, and I am likely to be busier still[1] this evening. By the way, Doctor, I shall want your co-operation.'

'I shall be delighted.'

'You don't mind breaking the law[2]?'

'Not in the least[3].'

'Nor running a chance of arrest[4]?'

'Not in a good cause.'

'Oh, the cause is excellent!'

'Then I am your man.'

'I was sure that I might rely[5] on you.'

'But what is it you wish?'

'When Mrs. Turner has[6] brought in the tray I will make it clear to you. Now,' he said, as he turned hungrily on the simple fare[7] that our landlady had provided, 'I must discuss it while I eat, for[8] I have not much time. It is nearly five now. In two hours we must be on the scene of action. Miss Irene, or Madame, rather, returns from her drive[9] at seven. We must be at Briony Lodge to meet her.'

'And what then?'

'You must leave that to me[10]. I have already arranged what is to occur[11]. There is only one point on which I must insist. You must not interfere[12], come what may[13]. You understand?'

'I am to be neutral?'

'To do nothing whatever. There will probably be some small unpleasantness[14]. Do not join in it[15]. It will end in my being conveyed[16] into the house. Four or five minutes afterwards the sitting-room window will open. You are to station yourself[17] close to[18] that open window.'

'Yes.'

'You are to watch me, for I will be visible to you.'

'Yes.'

1. il est probable que je le serai encore plus
2. d'enfreindre la loi
3. Pas le moins du monde
4. Ni de risquer de vous faire arrêter
5. compter
6. aura
7. collation
8. car
9. promenade
10. Laissez-moi faire
11. prévu la suite
12. intervenir
13. quoi qu'il arrive
14. un léger désagrément
15. Ne vous en mêlez pas
16. En fin de compte je serai transporté
17. vous positionner
18. près de

'And when I raise my hand – so – you will throw into the room what I give you to throw, and will, at the same time, raise the cry of fire[1]. You quite follow me?'

'Entirely.'

'It is nothing very formidable[2],' he said, taking a long cigar-shaped roll[3] from his pocket. 'It is an ordinary plumber's smoke rocket[4], fitted with[5] a cap at either end to make it self-lighting[6]. Your task is confined[7] to that. When you raise your cry of fire, it will be taken up by quite a number of people[8]. You may then walk to the end of the street, and I will rejoin you in ten minutes. I hope that I have made myself clear?'

'I am to remain neutral, to get near the window, to watch you, and, at the signal, to throw in this object, then to raise the cry of fire, and to await you at the corner of the street.'

'Precisely.'

'Then you may entirely rely on me.'

'That is excellent. I think perhaps it is almost time that I prepared for the new rôle I have to play.'

He disappeared into his bedroom, and returned in a few minutes in the character[9] of an amiable and simple-minded[10] Nonconformist clergyman. His broad black hat, his baggy[11] trousers, his white tie, his sympathetic smile, and general look of peering[12] and benevolent[13] curiosity, were such as Mr. John Hare alone could have equalled[14]. It was not merely[15] that Holmes changed his costume. His expression, his manner, his very soul[16] seemed to vary with every fresh part[17] that he assumed[18]. The stage[19] lost a fine actor, even as[20] science lost an acute reasoner, when he became a specialist in crime.

1. crier au feu
2. impressionnant
3. rouleau en forme de cigare
4. fusée fumigène de plombier
5. pourvue d'
6. une capsule d'auto-allumage à chaque extrémité
7. se borne
8. bien des gens vont faire de même
9. sous l'aspect
10. simplet
11. flottant
12. scrutatrice
13. bienveillante
14. seul Mr. John Hare [acteur] aurait pu les égaler
15. seulement
16. son âme même
17. nouveau rôle
18. endossait
19. théâtre
20. de même que

It was a quarter past six when we left Baker Street, and it still wanted ten minutes to the hour[1] when we found ourselves in Serpentine Avenue. It was already dusk[2], and the lamps were just being lighted as we paced up and down in front of Briony Lodge, waiting for the coming of its occupant. The house was just such as I had pictured it[3] from Sherlock Holmes's succinct description, but the locality[4] appeared to be less private[5] than I expected. On the contrary, for a small street in a quiet neighbourhood[6], it was remarkably animated. There was a group of shabbily-dressed[7] men smoking and laughing in a corner, a scissors-grinder[8] with his wheel, two guardsmen who were flirting with a nurse-girl, and several well-dressed young men who were lounging up and down[9] with cigars in their mouths.

'You see,' remarked Holmes, as we paced to and fro[10] in front of the house, 'this marriage rather simplifies matters. The photograph becomes a double-edged weapon[11] now. The chances are[12] that she would be as averse[13] to its being seen by Mr. Godfrey Norton[14], as our client is to its coming to the eyes of his Princess. Now the question is – Where are we to find the photograph?'

'Where, indeed?'

'It is most unlikely[15] that she carries it about with her[16]. It is cabinet size. Too large for easy concealment about a woman's dress. She knows that the King is capable of having her waylaid[17] and searched[18]. Two attempts of the sort have already been made. We may take it then[19] that she does not carry it about with her.'

'Where, then?'

'Her banker or her lawyer. There is that double possibility. But I am inclined to think neither[20]. Women are naturally secretive[21], and they like to

1. il était encore moins dix
2. le crépuscule
3. telle que je me l'étais représentée
4. l'endroit
5. isolé
6. quartier
7. pauvrement vêtus
8. rémouleur
9. se promenaient
10. faisions les cent pas
11. arme à double tranchant
12. Il y a de fortes chances
13. répugne
14. à ce que Mr. Godfrey Norton la voie
15. improbable
16. sur elle
17. la faire intercepter
18. fouiller
19. donc supposer
20. qu'elle n'est ni chez l'un ni chez l'autre
21. de nature secrète

do their own secreting[1]. Why should she hand it over[2] to anyone else? She could trust her own guardianship[3], but she could not tell what indirect or political influence might be brought to bear upon[4] a business man. Besides, remember that she had resolved to use it within a few days. It must be where she can lay her hands upon it[5]. It must be in her own house.'

'But it has twice been burgled[6].'

'Pshaw[7]! They did not know how to look[8].'

'But how will you look?'

'I will not look.'

'What then?'

'I will get her to show me.'

'But she will refuse.'

'She will not be able to. But I hear the rumble[9] of wheels. It is her carriage. Now carry out my orders[10] to the letter.'

As he spoke, the gleam[11] of the sidelights[12] of a carriage came round the curve of the avenue. It was a smart[13] little landau which rattled up to[14] the door of Briony Lodge. As it pulled up[15], one of the loafing men[16] at the corner dashed forward to open the door in the hope of earning a copper[17], but was elbowed away[18] by another loafer who had rushed up with the same intention. A fierce[19] quarrel broke out, which was increased by the two guardsmen, who took sides with[20] one of the loungers, and by the scissors-grinder, who was equally hot upon the other side[21]. A blow was struck, and in an instant the lady, who had stepped from her carriage, was the centre of a little knot[22] of flushed and struggling men who struck savagely at each other with their fists[23] and sticks. Holmes dashed into the crowd to protect the lady; but just as he reached her, he gave a cry and dropped to the ground, with

1. ne s'en remettent à personne pour garder leurs secrets
2. l'aurait-elle remise
3. vigilance
4. amenée à peser sur
5. à portée de main
6. cambriolée
7. Peuh
8. chercher
9. grondement
10. suivez mes instructions
11. lueur
12. lanternes latérales
13. élégant
14. s'en vint dans un bruit de ferraille jusque devant
15. Quand il s'arrêta
16. traîne-savate
17. gagner un sou
18. écarté du coude
19. violente
20. prirent parti pour
21. soutint l'adversaire avec autant de véhémence
22. mêlée
23. à coups de poing

the blood running freely down his face. At his fall the guardsmen took to their heels[1] in one direction and the loungers in the other, while a number of better dressed people who had watched the scuffle[2] without taking part in it, crowded in[3] to help the lady and to attend to[4] the injured man[5]. Irene Adler, as I will still call her, had hurried up the steps; but she stood at the top with her superb figure[6] outlined[7] against the lights of the hall, looking back into the street.

'Is the poor gentleman much hurt?' she asked.

'He is dead,' cried several voices.

'No, no, there's life in him,' shouted another. 'But he'll be gone[8] before you can get him to hospital.'

'He's a brave fellow,' said a woman. 'They would have had the lady's purse[9] and watch if it hadn't been for him[10]. They were a gang, and a rough one[11], too[12]. Ah, he's breathing now.'

'He can't lie in the street. May we bring him in, marm[13]?'

'Surely. Bring him into the sitting-room. There is a comfortable sofa. This way, please!'

Slowly and solemnly he was borne[14] into Briony Lodge, and laid out in the principal room, while I still observed the proceedings[15] from my post by the window. The lamps had been lit, but the blinds had not been drawn, so that I could see Holmes as he lay upon the couch[16]. I do not know whether he was seized with compunction[17] at that moment for the part[18] he was playing, but I know that I never felt more heartily ashamed of myself in my life than when I saw the beautiful creature against whom I was conspiring, or the grace and kindliness[19] with which she waited upon[20] the injured man. And yet it would be the blackest[21] treachery to Holmes to draw back[22] now from the part[23] which he had

1. détalèrent
2. bagarre
3. s'attroupèrent
4. soigner
5. blessé
6. silhouette
7. se profilant
8. mort
9. sac
10. s'il n'était pas intervenu
11. une bande, et violente
12. en plus
13. [madam]
14. transporté
15. événements
16. canapé
17. pris de scrupules
18. comédie
19. gentillesse
20. soigna
21. la pire
22. de me départir
23. du rôle

entrusted to me[1]. I hardened my heart and took the smoke rocket from under my ulster[2]. After all, I thought, we are not injuring her. We are but preventing her[3] from injuring another[4].

Holmes had sat up upon the couch, and I saw him motion[5] like a man who is in want[6] of air. A maid rushed across and threw open the window. At the same instant I saw him raise his hand, and at the signal I tossed my rocket into the room with a cry of 'Fire.' The word was no sooner out of my mouth than[7] the whole crowd of spectators, well dressed and ill[8] – gentlemen, ostlers[9], and servant maids – joined in a general shriek of[10] 'Fire.' Thick clouds of smoke curled through the room, and out at the open window. I caught a glimpse of rushing figures[11], and a moment later the voice of Holmes from within, assuring them that it was a false alarm. Slipping through the shouting crowd I made my way to the corner of the street, and in ten minutes was rejoiced[12] to find my friend's arm in mine, and to get away from the scene of the uproar[13]. He walked swiftly and in silence for some few minutes, until we had turned down[14] one of the quiet streets which lead towards the Edgware Road.

'You did it very nicely[15], Doctor,' he remarked. 'Nothing could have been better. It is all right.'

'You have the photograph!'

'I know where it is.'

'And how did you find out?'

'She showed me, as I told you that she would.'

'I am still in the dark[16].'

'I do not wish to make a mystery,' said he, laughing. 'The matter was perfectly simple. You, of course, saw that every one in the street was an accomplice[17]. They were all engaged for the evening.'

'I guessed as much[18].'

1. m'avait confié
2. pardessus
3. ne faisons que l'empêcher
4. de nuire à un autre
5. faire des gestes
6. manque
7. que
8. bien ou mal vêtus
9. valets d'écurie
10. se mirent en chœur à crier
11. silhouettes
12. me réjouis
13. tumulte
14. dans
15. avez parfaitement joué votre rôle
16. Je n'y comprends toujours rien
17. complices
18. m'en suis douté

'Then, when the row[1] broke out[2], I had a little moist[3] red paint in the palm of my hand. I rushed forward, fell down, clapped my hand to my face, and became a piteous[4] spectacle. It is an old trick[5].'

'That also I could fathom[6].'

'Then they carried me in. She was bound[7] to have me in. What else could she do? And into her sitting-room, which was the very room which[8] I suspected. It lay between that and her bedroom, and I was determined to see which. They laid me on a couch, I motioned for air, they were compelled[9] to open the window and you had your chance.'

'How did that help you?'

'It was all-important[10]. When a woman thinks that her house is on fire, her instinct is at once to rush to the thing which she values most[11]. It is a perfectly overpowering[12] impulse, and I have more than once taken advantage of it[13]. In the case of the Darlington Substitution Scandal it was of use to me, and also in the Arnsworth Castle business. A married woman grabs at[14] her baby – an unmarried one reaches for[15] her jewel box. Now it was clear to me that our lady of today had nothing in the house more precious to her than what we are in quest of[16]. She would rush to secure it[17]. The alarm of fire was admirably done. The smoke and shouting was enough to shake nerves of steel. She responded beautifully. The photograph is in a recess[18] behind a sliding panel[19] just above the right bell-pull[20]. She was there in an instant, and I caught a glimpse of it as she half drew it out. When I cried out that it was a false alarm, she replaced it, glanced at the rocket, rushed from the room, and I have not seen her since. I rose, and, making my excuses, escaped from the house. I hesitated whether to attempt to secure[21] the photograph at once; but the coachman had come in, and as he was watching

1. algarade
2. a débuté
3. humide
4. pitoyable
5. ruse
6. le deviner
7. obligée
8. la pièce que précisément
9. contraints
10. essentiel
11. ce à quoi elle tient le plus
12. incontrôlable
13. j'en ai plus d'une fois tiré parti
14. empoigne
15. veut se saisir de
16. nous recherchons
17. le mettre à l'abri
18. renfoncement
19. panneau coulissant
20. cordon de la sonnette de droite
21. à m'emparer

me narrowly[1], it seemed safer to wait. A little over-precipitance[2] may ruin all.'

'And now?' I asked.

'Our quest is practically finished. I shall call with[3] the King tomorrow, and with you, if you care to come with us. We will be shown[4] into the sitting-room to wait for the lady, but it is probable that when she comes she may find neither us nor the photograph. It might be a satisfaction to His Majesty to regain it[5] with his own hands.'

'And when will you call?'

'At eight in the morning. She will not be up[6], so that we shall have a clear field[7]. Besides, we must be prompt, for[8] this marriage may mean a complete change in her life and habits. I must wire[9] to the King without delay.'

We had reached Baker Street, and had stopped at the door. He was searching his pockets for the key, when someone passing said:

'Good night, Mister Sherlock Holmes.'

There were several people on the pavement at the time, but the greeting appeared to come from a slim[10] youth[11] in an ulster who had hurried by[12].

'I've heard that voice before,' said Holmes, staring down the dimly lit[13] street. 'Now, I wonder[14] who the deuce[15] that could have been.'

I slept at Baker Street that night, and we were engaged upon[16] our toast and coffee when the King of Bohemia rushed into the room.

'You have really got it!' he cried, grasping[17] Sherlock Holmes by either shoulder[18], and looking eagerly into his face[19].

'Not yet.'

'But you have hopes?'

'I have hopes.'

1. de près
2. excès de précipitation
3. irai voir
4. On nous conduira
5. d'en reprendre possession
6. levée
7. le champ libre
8. car
9. câbler
10. svelte
11. jeune homme
12. était passé à la hâte
13. mal éclairée
14. Je me demande bien
15. qui diable
16. prenions
17. empoignant
18. les deux épaules
19. en le dévisageant intensément

'Then, come. I am all impatience to be gone.'

'We must have a cab.'

'No, my brougham is waiting.'

'Then that will simplify matters.'

We descended, and started off[1] once more for Briony Lodge.

'Irene Adler is married,' remarked Holmes.

'Married! When?'

'Yesterday.'

'But to whom?'

'To an English lawyer named Norton.'

'But she could not love him[2]?'

'I am in hopes that she does[3].'

'And why in hopes?'

'Because it would spare[4] Your Majesty all fear of future annoyance. If the lady loves her husband, she does not love Your Majesty. If she does not love Your Majesty there is no reason why she should interfere with[5] Your Majesty's plan.'

'It is true. And yet! Well! I wish she had been of my own station[6]! What a queen she would have made!' He relapsed[7] into a moody[8] silence which was not broken until we drew up[9] in Serpentine Avenue.

The door of Briony Lodge was open, and an elderly[10] woman stood upon the steps. She watched us with a sardonic eye as we stepped from the brougham.

'Mr. Sherlock Holmes, I believe?' said she.

'I am Mr. Holmes,' answered my companion, looking at her with a questioning and rather startled[11] gaze.

'Indeed! My mistress told me that you were likely to call[12]. She left this morning with her husband, by the 5.15 train from Charing Cross, for the Continent.'

1. partîmes
2. ne peut pas être amoureuse de lui
3. J'ai dans l'espoir que si
4. épargnerait à
5. qu'elle contrarie
6. rang
7. retomba
8. maussade
9. notre arrêt
10. âgée
11. surpris
12. passeriez probablement

'What!' Sherlock Holmes staggered back[1], white with chagrin and surprise. 'Do you mean that she has left England?'

'Never to return[2].'

'And the papers?' asked the King hoarsely[3]. 'All is lost.'

'We shall see.' He pushed past the servant, and rushed into the drawing-room, followed by the King and myself. The furniture[4] was scattered about[5] in every direction, with dismantled shelves[6], and open drawers, as if the lady had hurriedly ransacked them[7] before her flight[8]. Holmes rushed at the bell-pull, tore back[9] a small sliding[10] shutter[11], and, plunging in his hand, pulled out a photograph and a letter. The photograph was of Irene Adler herself in evening dress, the letter was superscribed[12] to 'Sherlock Holmes, Esq. To be left till called for[13].' My friend tore it open and we all three read it together. It was dated at midnight of the preceding night, and ran in this way[14]:–

MY DEAR MR. SHERLOCK HOLMES,

You really did it very well. You took me in completely[15]. Until after the alarm of fire, I had not a suspicion. But then, when I found how I had betrayed myself[16], I began to think. I had been warned against you[17] months ago. I had been told that if the King employed an agent, it would certainly be you. And your address had been given me. Yet, with[18] all this, you made me reveal what you wanted to know. Even after I became suspicious[19], I found it hard to think evil[20] of such a dear, kind old clergyman. But, you know, I have been trained[21] as an actress[22] myself. Male costume[23] is nothing new to me. I often take

1. recula en chancelant
2. Et ne reviendra pas
3. d'une voix rauque
4. Les meubles
5. éparpillés
6. leurs étagères démontées
7. tout mis sens dessus dessous
8. fuite
9. fit glisser brutalement
10. coulissant
11. panneau
12. adressée
13. Son destinataire passera la prendre
14. était rédigée ainsi
15. J'ai été votre dupe de bout en bout
16. m'étais trahie
17. On m'avait mise en garde contre vous
18. malgré
19. méfiante
20. penser en mal
21. formée
22. au métier d'actrice
23. déguisement

advantage of the freedom which it gives. I sent John, the coachman, to watch you, ran upstairs, got into my walking clothes, as I call them, and came down just as you departed. Well, I followed you to your door, and so made sure[1] that I was really an object of interest to the celebrated[2] Mr. Sherlock Holmes. Then I, rather imprudently, wished you good night, and started for the Temple to see my husband. We both thought the best resource[3] was flight when pursued[4] by so formidable an antagonist[5]; so you will find the nest empty when you call tomorrow. As to the photograph, your client may rest in peace[6]. I love and am loved by a better man than he. The King may do what he will [7]without hindrance[8] from one whom he has cruelly wronged[9]. I keep it only to safeguard myself[10], and to preserve a weapon[11] which will always secure me from[12] any steps[13] which he might take in the future. I leave a photograph which he might care[14] to possess; and I remain, dear Mr. Sherlock Holmes, very truly yours,

IRENE NORTON, née ADLER.

'What a woman – oh, what a woman!' cried the King of Bohemia, when we had all three read this epistle[15]. 'Did I not tell you how quick and resolute she was? Would she not have made an admirable queen? Is it not a pity she was not on my level?'

'From what I have seen of the lady, she seems, indeed, to be on a very different level to Your Majesty,' said Holmes, coldly. 'I am sorry that I have not been able to bring Your Majesty's business to a more successful conclusion.'

1. m'assurai
2. fameux
3. parti
4. on est poursuivi
5. un adversaire aussi redoutable
6. se tranquilliser
7. à sa guise
8. tracasserie
9. à qui il a fait beaucoup de tort
10. pour me protéger
11. me garder une arme
12. me prémunira toujours contre
13. toute mesure
14. qu'il lui plaira peut-être
15. missive

'On the contrary, my dear sir,' cried the King. 'Nothing could be more successful. I know that her word is inviolate[1]. The photograph is now as safe as if it were in the fire.'

'I am glad to hear Your Majesty say so.'

'I am immensely indebted[2] to you. Pray tell me in what way I can reward you[3]. This ring–' He slipped an emerald snake ring from his finger and held it out upon the palm of his hand.

'Your Majesty has something which I should value even more highly[4],' said Holmes.

'You have but to name it[5].'

'This photograph!'

The King stared at him in amazement.

'Irene's photograph!' he cried. 'Certainly, if you wish it.'

'I thank Your Majesty. Then there is no more to be done in the matter. I have the honour to wish you a very good morning.' He bowed[6], and, turning away without observing the hand which the King had stretched out to him[7], he set off in my company for his chambers.

And that was how a great scandal threatened to affect the kingdom of Bohemia, and how the best plans of Mr. Sherlock Holmes were beaten[8] by a woman's wit[9]. He used to make merry over[10] the cleverness of women, but I have not heard him do it of late[11]. And when he speaks of Irene Adler, or when he refers to her photograph, it is always under the honourable title of *the* woman.

1. sa parole est sacrée
2. redevable
3. vous récompenser
4. qui serait plus précieux encore à mes yeux
5. Dites seulement
6. s'inclina
7. lui tendait
8. déjoués
9. la vivacité d'esprit
10. se moquer de
11. ces temps derniers

The Five Orange Pips[1]

1. pépins d'orange

Sherlock Holmes peut-il briser la malédiction qui pèse sur les Openshaw ? Ils semblent en effet promis à une mort certaine dès qu'ils ont reçu par la poste cinq curieux pépins d'orange.

WHEN I GLANCE over[1] my notes and records[2] of the Sherlock Holmes cases[3] between the years '82 and '90, I am faced by[4] so many which present strange and interesting features[5], that it is no easy matter to know which to choose and which to leave. Some, however, have already gained publicity through the papers[6], and others have not offered a field for those peculiar qualities which my friend possessed in so high a degree, and which it is the object of these papers to illustrate. Some, too, have baffled[7] his analytical skill[8], and would be, as narratives[9], beginnings without an ending, while others have been but partially cleared up[10], and have their explanations founded rather upon conjecture and surmise[11] than on that absolute logical proof which was so dear to him. There is, however, one of these last which was so remarkable in its details and so startling[12] in its results, that I am tempted to give some account of it[13], in spite of the fact that there are points in connection with it which never have been, and probably never will be, entirely cleared up.

The year '87 furnished us with a long series of cases of greater or less interest, of which I retain the records. Among my headings[14] under this one twelve months[15], I find an account of the adventure of the Paradol Chamber, of the Amateur Mendicant[16] Society, who held a luxurious[17] club in the lower vault[18] of a furniture warehouse[19], of the facts connected with the loss of the British barque[20] *Sophy Anderson*, of the singular adventures of the Grice Patersons in the island of Uffa, and finally of the Camberwell poisoning case. In the latter, as may be remembered, Sherlock Holmes was able, by winding up[21] the dead man's watch, to prove that it

1. consulte
2. archives
3. affaires
4. confronté à
5. traits
6. journaux
7. mis en défaut
8. talent
9. en tant que récits
10. n'ont été que partiellement élucidées
11. les suppositions
12. surprenante
13. d'en faire le récit
14. rubriques
15. de cette année-là
16. mendiante
17. luxueux
18. salle basse voûtée
19. magasin d'ameublement
20. trois-mâts
21. en remontant

had been wound up two hours ago, and that therefore[1] the deceased[2] had gone to bed within that time[3] – a deduction which was of the greatest importance in clearing up[4] the case. All these I may sketch out[5] at some future date, but none of them present such singular features as the strange train of circumstances which I have now taken up my pen to describe.

It was in the latter[6] days of September, and the equinoctial gales[7] had set in[8] with exceptional violence. All day the wind had screamed and the rain had beaten against the windows, so that even here in the heart of great, hand-made[9] London we were forced to raise our minds for the instant from the routine of life, and to recognize the presence of those great elemental[10] forces which shriek at mankind[11] through the bars[12] of his civilization, like untamed[13] beasts in a cage. As evening drew in[14] the storm grew louder and louder, and the wind cried and sobbed[15] like a child in the chimney. Sherlock Holmes sat moodily[16] at one side of the fireplace cross-indexing[17] his records of crime, whilst[18] I at the other was deep in one of Clark Russell's fine sea stories, until the howl[19] of the gale from without seemed to blend[20] with the text, and the splash of the rain to lengthen out[21] into the long swash[22] of the sea waves. My wife was on a visit to her aunt's, and for a few days I was a dweller[23] once more in my old quarters[24] at Baker Street.

'Why,[25]' said I, glancing up[26] at my companion, 'that was surely the bell? Who could come tonight? Some friend of yours, perhaps?'

'Except yourself I have none,' he answered. 'I do not encourage visitors.'

'A client, then?'

1. par conséquent
2. défunt
3. dans ce laps de temps
4. dans la résolution de
5. retracerai peut-être
6. derniers
7. tempêtes d'équinoxe
8. étaient survenues
9. construite par l'homme
10. de la nature
11. hurlent à la face de l'humanité
12. barreaux
13. indomptées
14. À tombée de la nuit,
15. sanglota
16. morose
17. établissant les renvois sur
18. tandis que
19. hurlement
20. se fondre
21. se prolonger
22. froufrou
23. j'habitais
24. logement
25. Mais
26. levant les yeux

'If so, it is a serious case. Nothing less would bring a man out on such a day, and at such an hour. But I take it that it is more likely[1] to be some crony[2] of the landlady's[3].'

Sherlock Holmes was wrong in his conjecture, however, for[4] there came a step[5] in the passage, and a tapping[6] at the door. He stretched out[7] his long arm to turn the lamp away from himself and towards the vacant chair upon which a newcomer[8] must sit. 'Come in!' said he.

The man who entered was young, some two-and-twenty at the outside[9], well groomed[10] and trimly[11] clad[12], with something of refinement and delicacy in his bearing[13]. The streaming[14] umbrella which he held in his hand, and his long shining waterproof[15] told of the fierce[16] weather through which he had come. He looked about him anxiously in the glare[17] of the lamp, and I could see that his face was pale and his eyes heavy, like those of a man who is weighed down with[18] some great anxiety.

'I owe you an apology[19],' he said, raising his golden pince-nez to his eyes. 'I trust[20] that I am not intruding[21]. I fear that I have brought some traces of the storm and the rain into your snug[22] chamber.'

'Give me your coat and umbrella,' said Holmes. 'They may rest here on the hook[23], and will be dry presently[24]. You have come up from the south-west, I see.'

'Yes, from Horsham.'

'That clay[25] and chalk[26] mixture which I see upon your toecaps[27] is quite distinctive[28]:

'I have come for advice.'

'That is easily got.'

'And help.'

'That is not always so easy.'

1. il s'agit sans doute plutôt
2. d'une amie
3. la logeuse
4. car
5. on entendit des pas
6. frapper
7. tendit
8. nouveau venu
9. tout au plus
10. impeccable
11. avec soin
12. vêtu
13. maintien
14. ruisselant
15. imperméable
16. exécrable
17. éclat aveuglant
18. qu'accable
19. vous dois des excuses
20. J'espère
21. ne dérange pas
22. confortable
23. patère
24. bientôt
25. d'argile
26. de craie
27. au bout de vos chaussures
28. caractéristique

'I have heard of you, Mr. Holmes. I heard from Major Prendergast how you saved him in the Tankerville Club Scandal.'

1. à tort
2. d'avoir triché

'Ah, of course. He was wrongfully[1] accused of cheating[2] at cards.'

'He said that you could solve anything.'

'He said too much.'

'That you are never beaten.'

'I have been beaten four times – three times by men and once by a woman.'

'But what is that compared with the number of your successes?'

'It is true that I have been generally successful.'

'Then you may be so with me.'

3. Je vous en prie, approchez
4. accordez-moi

'I beg that you will draw[3] your chair up to the fire, and favour me with[4] some details as to your case.'

'It is no ordinary one.'

5. recours

'None of those which come to me are. I am the last court of appeal[5].'

6. me demande
7. si
8. série d'événements

'And yet I question[6], sir, whether[7], in all your experience, you have ever listened to a more mysterious and inexplicable chain of events[8] than those which have happened in my own family.'

9. sur les

'You fill me with interest,' said Holmes. 'Pray give us the essential facts from the commencement, and I can afterwards question you as to those[9] details which seem to me to be most important.'

10. les flammes

The young man pulled his chair up, and pushed his wet feet out towards the blaze[10].

11. pour autant que

'My name,' said he, 'is John Openshaw, but my own affairs have, so far as[11] I can understand it, little to do with this awful business. It is a hereditary matter, so in order to give you an idea of the facts, I must go back to the commencement of the affair.

'You must know that my grandfather had two sons – my uncle Elias and my father Joseph. My father had a small factory at Coventry, which he enlarged[1] at the time of the invention of bicycling. He was the patentee[2] of the Openshaw unbreakable tyre[3], and his business met with[4] such success that he was able to sell it, and to retire[5] upon a handsome competence[6].

'My uncle Elias emigrated to America when he was a young man, and became a planter in Florida, where he was reported to have done very well[7]. At the time of the war[8] he fought in Jackson's army, and afterwards under Hood, where he rose to be a[9] colonel. When Lee laid down his arms my uncle returned to his plantation, where he remained for three or four years. About 1869 or 1870 he came back to Europe, and took a small estate[10] in Sussex, near Horsham. He had made a very considerable fortune in the States, and his reason for leaving them was his aversion to the negroes[11], and his dislike of the Republican policy[12] in extending the franchise to them[13]. He was a singular man, fierce[14] and quick-tempered[15], very foul-mouthed[16] when he was angry, and of a most retiring disposition[17]. During all the years that he lived at Horsham I doubt if ever he set foot in the town. He had a garden and two or three fields round his house, and there he would take his exercise, though very often for weeks on end he would never leave his room. He drank a great deal of brandy, and smoked very heavily[18], but he would see no society[19], and did not want any friends, not even his own brother.

'He didn't mind me[20], in fact he took a fancy to me[21], for at the time when he saw me first I was a youngster of twelve or so. That would be in the year 1878, after he had been eight or nine years in England.

1. a agrandie

2. détenteur du brevet

3. pneu increvable

4. a connu

5. prendre sa retraite

6. des revenus très confortables

7. où, dit-on, il a fort bien réussi

8. [guerre de Sécession]

9. a atteint le grade de

10. propriété

11. envers les Noirs

12. politique

13. qui leur octroyait la liberté

14. violent

15. colérique

16. grossier

17. très enclin à la solitude

18. énormément

19. ne voulait voir personne

20. Ma présence ne le dérangeait pas

21. m'a pris en affection

He begged[1] my father to let me live with him, and he was very kind to me in his way. When he was sober he used to be fond of playing backgammon and draughts[2] with me, and he would make me his representative both with the servants and with the tradespeople[3], so that by the time that I was sixteen I was quite master of the house. I kept all the keys, and could go where I liked and do what I liked, so long as I did not disturb him in his privacy[4]. There was one singular exception, however, for he had a single room, a lumber-room[5] up among the attics[6], which was invariably locked, and which he would never permit either me or anyone else to enter. With a boy's curiosity I have peeped through the keyhole[7], but I was never able to see more than such a collection[8] of old trunks[9] and bundles[10] as would be expected[11] in such a room.

'One day – it was in March, 1883 – a letter with a foreign stamp lay upon the table in front of the Colonel's plate. It was not a common thing for him to receive letters, for[12] his bills[13] were all paid in ready money[14], and he had no friends of any sort. "From India!" said he, as he took it up, "Pondicherry postmark! What can this be?" Opening it hurriedly, out there jumped five little dried orange pips, which pattered down upon his plate[15]. I began to laugh at this, but the laugh was struck[16] from my lips at the sight of his face. His lip had fallen, his eyes were protruding[17], his skin the colour of putty[18], and he glared[19] at the envelope which he still held in his trembling hand. "K. K. K.," he shrieked, and then: "My God, my God, my sins[20] have overtaken me[21]."

" 'What is it, uncle!" I cried.

" 'Death," said he, and rising from the table he retired to his room, leaving me palpitating with horror. I took up the envelope, and saw scrawled[22] in

1. a imploré
2. aux dames
3. commerçants
4. intimité
5. débarras
6. grenier
7. essayé de regarder par le trou de la serrure
8. le bric-à-brac
9. malles
10. paquets
11. auquel on peut s'attendre
12. car
13. factures
14. en liquide
15. sont tombés sur son assiette en tintant
16. s'est effacé
17. exorbités
18. d'un gris jaunâtre
19. lançait un regard noir
20. péchés
21. m'ont rattrapé
22. griffonnée

red ink upon the inner flap[1], just above the gum[2], the letter K three times repeated. There was nothing else save[3] the five dried pips. What could be the reason of his overpowering[4] terror? I left the breakfast-table, and as I ascended the stairs I met him coming down with an old rusty[5] key, which must have belonged to the attic, in one hand, and a small brass[6] box, like a cash box, in the other.

" 'They may do what they like, but I'll checkmate them still[7]," said he, with an oath[8]. "Tell Mary that I shall want a fire in my room today, and send down to[9] Fordham, the Horsham lawyer[10]."

'I did as he ordered, and when the lawyer arrived I was asked to step up[11] to the room. The fire was burning brightly, and in the grate[12] there was a mass of black, fluffy[13] ashes, as of burned paper, while the brass box stood open and empty beside it. As I glanced at the box I noticed, with a start[14], that upon the lid were printed the treble K which I had read in the morning upon the envelope.

" 'I wish you, John," said my uncle, "to witness[15] my will[16]. I leave my estate, with all its advantages and all its disadvantages to my brother, your father, whence it will, no doubt, descend to you. If you can enjoy it[17] in peace, well and good! If you find you cannot, take my advice[18], my boy, and leave it to your deadliest[19] enemy. I am sorry to give you such a two-edged thing[20], but I can't say what turn[21] things are going to take. Kindly sign the paper where Mr. Fordham shows you."

'I signed the paper as directed, and the lawyer took it away with him. The singular incident made, as you may think, the deepest impression upon me, and I pondered over it[22], and turned it every way in my mind without being able to make anything of it. Yet I could not shake off the[23] vague feeling of

1. rabat intérieur
2. colle
3. hormis
4. insurmontable
5. rouillée
6. en cuivre
7. les tiendrai tout de même en échec
8. juron
9. envoyez chercher
10. notaire
11. de monter
12. âtre
13. duveteuses
14. tressaillement
15. que tu sois témoin de
16. testament
17. en jouir
18. suis mon conseil
19. le plus mortel
20. de te faire ce don à double tranchant
21. tournure
22. j'y ai réfléchi
23. me débarrasser du

dread[1] which it left behind it, though the sensation grew less keen[2] as the weeks passed, and nothing happened to disturb the usual routine of our lives. I could see a change in my uncle, however. He drank more than ever, and he was less inclined for any sort of society. Most of his time he would spend in his room, with the door locked upon the inside, but sometimes he would emerge in a sort of drunken frenzy[3] and would burst out of the house and tear about[4] the garden with a revolver in his hand, screaming out that he was afraid of no man, and that he was not to be cooped up[5], like a sheep in a pen[6], by man or devil. When these hot fits[7] were over, however, he would rush tumultuously in at the door, and lock and bar it[8] behind him, like a man who can brazen it out no longer against[9] the terror which lies at the roots of his soul. At such times I have seen his face even on a cold day, glisten with moisture[10] as though it were new raised[11] from a basin[12].

'Well, to come to an end of the matter, Mr. Holmes, and not to abuse your patience, there came a night when he made one of those drunken sallies[13] from which he never came back. We found him, when we went to search for him, face downwards in a little green-scummed[14] pool, which lay at the foot of the garden. There was no sign of any violence, and the water was but two feet deep[15], so that the jury[16], having regard to[17] his known eccentricity, brought in[18] a verdict of suicide. But I, who knew how he winced from the very thought[19] of death, had much ado[20] to persuade myself that he had gone out of his way to meet it[21]. The matter passed, however, and my father entered into possession of the estate, and of some fourteen thousand pounds, which lay to his credit at the bank.'

1. crainte
2. vive
3. ivresse frénétique
4. arpenter avec rage
5. n'allait pas se laisser enfermer
6. enclos
7. violentes crises
8. fermer à double tour
9. ne peut plus affronter crânement
10. couvert d'une sueur luisante
11. venait de sortir
12. cuvette
13. sorties enivrées
14. couverte d'écume verte
15. n'avait que 60 cm de profondeur
16. [lié au coroner, il doit déterminer les causes d'un décès]
17. tenant compte de
18. rendit
19. répugnait à l'idée même
20. j'avais beaucoup de mal
21. l'eût cherchée

'One moment,' Holmes interposed. 'Your statement is, I foresee[1], one of the most remarkable to which I have ever listened. Let me have the date of the reception by your uncle of the letter, and the date of his supposed suicide.'

'The letter arrived on March the 10th, 1883. His death was seven weeks later, upon the night of the 2nd of May.'

'Thank you. Pray proceed[2].'

'When my father took over[3] the Horsham property, he, at my request, made a careful examination of the attic, which had been always locked up. We found the brass box there, although its contents[4] had been destroyed. On the inside of the cover was a paper label[5], with the initials K. K. K. repeated upon it, and "Letters, memoranda, receipts[6] and a register" written beneath. These, we presume, indicated the nature of the papers which had been destroyed by Colonel Openshaw. For the rest, there was nothing of much importance in the attic, save a great many scattered papers and notebooks bearing upon[7] my uncle's life in America. Some of them were of the war time, and showed that he had done his duty well, and had borne the repute of being a[8] brave soldier. Others were of a date during the reconstruction of the Southern States, and were mostly concerned with politics, for he had evidently taken a strong part[9] in opposing the carpet-bag[10] politicians who had been sent down from the North.

'Well, it was the beginning of '84, when my father came to live at Horsham, and all went as well as possible with us until the January of '85. On the fourth day after the New Year I heard my father give a sharp cry of surprise as we sat together at the breakfast-table. There he was, sitting with a newly

1. le vois déjà
2. Continuez, je vous prie
3. est entré en possession de
4. son contenu
5. étiquette
6. reçus
7. se rapportant à
8. acquis la réputation d'un
9. joué un rôle important
10. profiteurs

opened envelope in one hand and five dried orange pips in the out-stretched palm[1] of the other one. He had always laughed at what he called my cock-and-bull[2] story about the Colonel, but he looked very puzzled[3] and scared now that the same thing had come upon himself.

" 'Why, what on earth does this mean[4], John?" he stammered[5].

'My heart had turned to lead[6]. "It is K. K. K.," said I.

'He looked inside the envelope. "So it is[7]," he cried. "Here are the very letters. But what is this written above them?"

" 'Put the papers on the sun-dial[8]," I read, peeping[9] over his shoulder.

" 'What papers? What sun-dial?" he asked.

" 'The sun-dial in the garden. There is no other," said I; "but the papers must be those that are destroyed."

" 'Pooh!" said he, gripping hard[10] at his courage.' "We are in a civilized land here, and we can't have tomfoolery[11] of this kind. Where does the thing come from?"

" 'From Dundee," I answered, glancing at the postmark.

" 'Some preposterous[12] practical joke[13]," said he. "What have I to do with sun-dials and papers? I shall take no notice[14] of such nonsense."

" 'I should certainly speak to the police," I said.

" 'And be laughed at for my pains[15]. Nothing of the sort."

" 'Then let me do so."

" 'No, I forbid you. I won't have a fuss made[16] over such nonsense."

1. paume ouverte
2. à dormir debout
3. perplexe
4. Mais qu'est-ce que c'est que ça
5. bredouilla-t-il
6. Mon sang se glaça
7. En effet
8. cadran solaire
9. en regardant
10. se raccrochant de toutes ses forces
11. des absurdités
12. grotesque
13. farce
14. ne tiendrai aucun compte
15. qu'on me rie au nez
16. ne veux pas qu'on fasse d'histoires

'It was in vain to argue with him, for he was a very obstinate man. I went about, however, with a heart which was full of forebodings[1].

'On the third day after the coming of the letter my father went from home to visit an old friend of his, Major Freebody, who is in command of one of the forts upon Portsdown Hill. I was glad that he should go, for it seemed to me that he was further from danger[2] when he was away from home. In that, however, I was in error. Upon the second day of his absence I received a telegram from the Major, imploring me to come at once. My father had fallen over one of the deep chalk-pits[3] which abound in the neighbourhood, and was lying senseless[4], with a shattered skull[5]. I hurried to him, but he passed away[6] without having ever recovered his consciousness[7]. He had, as it appears, been returning from Fareham in the twilight, and as the country was unknown to him, and the chalk-pit unfenced[8], the jury had no hesitation in bringing in a verdict of "Death from accidental causes". Carefully as[9] I examined every fact connected with his death, I was unable to find anything which could suggest the idea of murder. There were no signs of violence, no footmarks, no robbery, no record of strangers[10] having been seen upon the roads. And yet I need not tell you that my mind was far from at ease[11], and that I was well-nigh[12] certain that some foul[13] plot[14] had been woven[15] round him.

'In this sinister way I came into my inheritance. You will ask me why I did not dispose of it[16]? I answer because I was well convinced that our troubles were in some way dependent upon[17] an incident in my uncle's life, and that the danger would be as pressing[18] in one house as in another.

1. d'appréhension
2. moins exposé
3. carrières de craie
4. inanimé
5. fracture du crâne
6. est mort
7. repris connaissance
8. non clôturée
9. Malgré le soin avec lequel
10. aucune trace d'inconnus
11. d'être serein
12. à peu près
13. odieuse
14. machination
15. s'était tramée
16. ne m'en suis pas débarrassé
17. dus à
18. important

'It was in January, '85, that my poor father met his end[1], and two years and eight months have elapsed[2] since then. During that time I have lived happily at Horsham, and I had begun to hope that this curse[3] had passed away from[4] the family, and that it had ended with the last[5] generation. I had begun to take comfort[6] too soon, however; yesterday morning the blow fell in the very shape in which it had come upon[7] my father.'

The young man took from his waistcoat[8] a crumpled[9] envelope, and, turning to the table, he shook out upon it five little dried orange pips.

'This is the envelope,' he continued. 'The postmark is London – eastern division[10]. Within are the very words[11] which were upon my father's last message. "K. K. K."; and then "Put the papers on the sundial".'

'What have you done?' asked Holmes.

'Nothing.'

'Nothing?'

'To tell the truth' – he sank[12] his face into his thin, white hands – 'I have felt helpless[13]. I have felt like one of those poor rabbits when the snake is writhing towards it[14]. I seem to be in the grasp of[15] some resistless, inexorable evil[16], which no foresight and no precautions can guard against[17].'

'Tut! Tut[18]!' cried Sherlock Holmes. 'You must act, man, or you are lost. Nothing but[19] energy can save you. This is no time for despair.'

'I have seen the police.'

'Ah?'

'But they listened to my story with a smile. I am convinced that the inspector has formed the opinion that the letters are all practical jokes[20], and that the deaths of my relations[21] were really accidents,

1. est mort
2. se sont écoulés
3. malédiction
4. quitté
5. précédente
6. à me tranquilliser
7. sous la même forme qu'avec
8. gilet
9. froissée
10. secteur de l'est
11. exactement les mêmes
12. enfouit
13. complètement désemparé
14. avance vers lui en ondulant
15. sous l'emprise de
16. esprit malin
17. dont aucune anticipation ni précaution ne saurait prémunir
18. Taratata
19. Seule
20. des farces
21. des membres de ma famille

as the jury stated, and were not to be connected with the warnings[1].'

Holmes shook his clenched hands[2] in the air. 'Incredible imbecility!' he cried.

'They have, however, allowed me[3] a policeman, who may remain in the house with me.'

'Has he come with you tonight?'

'No. His orders were to stay in the house.'

Again Holmes raved[4] in the air.

'Why did you come to me?' he said; 'and, above all, why did you not come at once?'

'I did not know. It was only today that I spoke to Major Prendergast about my trouble, and was advised by him to come to you.'

'It is really two days since you had the letter. We should have acted before this. You have no further evidence[5], I suppose, than that which you have placed before us – no suggestive[6] detail which might help us?'

'There is one thing,' said John Openshaw. He rummaged[7] in his coat pocket, and drawing out a piece of discoloured, blue-tinted paper, he laid it out upon the table. 'I have some remembrance,' said he, 'that on the day when my uncle burned the papers I observed that the small, unburned margins[8] which lay amid the ashes were of this particular colour. I found this single sheet[9] upon the floor of his room, and I am inclined to think that it may be one of the papers which had, perhaps, fluttered out from among the[10] others, and in that way escaped destruction. Beyond[11] the mention of pips, I do not see that it helps us much. I think myself that it is a page from some private diary[12]. The writing is undoubtedly my uncle's.'

Holmes moved the lamp, and we both bent over the sheet of paper, which showed by its

1. avertissements
2. poings
3. mis à ma disposition
4. agita les poings
5. d'autres preuves à l'appui
6. évocateur
7. fouilla
8. marges
9. feuillet
10. voltigé loin des
11. Mis à part
12. journal intime

1. bord irrégulier
2. En haut était inscrit
3. annotations
4. Pépins lancés sur
5. disparu [ou blanchi]

ragged edge[1] that it had indeed been torn from a book. It was headed[2] 'March, 1869', and beneath were the following enigmatical notices[3]:–

4th. Hudson came. Same old platform.

7th. Set the pips on[4] McCauley, Paramore, and John Swain of St Augustine.

9th. McCauley cleared[5].

10th. John Swain cleared.

12th. Visited Paramore. All well.

6. consacrer

'Thank you!' said Holmes, folding up the paper and returning it to our visitor. 'And now you must on no account lose another instant. We cannot spare[6] time even to discuss what you have told me. You must get home instantly, and act.'

'What shall I do?'

7. une seule chose
8. formuler cela
9. de façon convaincante
10. comme on vous le demande

'There is but one thing[7] to do. It must be done at once. You must put this piece of paper which you have shown us into the brass box which you have described. You must also put in a note to say that all the other papers were burned by your uncle, and that this is the only one which remains. You must assert that[8] in such words as will carry conviction with them[9]. Having done this, you must at once put the box out upon the sun-dial, as directed[10]. Do you understand?'

'Entirely.'

11. il nout faut tisser notre toile
12. tandis que
13. d'écarter
14. coupables

'Do not think of revenge, or anything of the sort, at present. I think that we may gain that by means of the law; but we have our web to weave[11], while[12] theirs is already woven. The first consideration is to remove[13] the pressing danger which threatens you. The second is to clear up the mystery, and to punish the guilty parties[14].'

'I thank you,' said the young man, rising, and pulling on his overcoat. 'You have given me fresh life and hope. I shall certainly do as you advise.'

'Do not lose an instant. And, above all, take care of yourself in the meanwhile[1], for I do not think that there can be a doubt that you are threatened by a very real and imminent danger. How do you go back?'

'By train from Waterloo.'

'It is not yet nine. The streets will be crowded, so I trust[2] that you may be in safety. And yet you cannot guard yourself too closely[3].'

'I am armed.'

'That is well. Tomorrow I shall set to work upon your case.'

'I shall see you at Horsham, then?'

'No, your secret lies in London. It is there that I shall seek it[4].

'Then I shall call upon you[5] in a day, or in two days, with news as to the box and the papers. I shall take your advice[6] in every particular[7].' He shook hands with us, and took his leave[8]. Outside the wind still screamed, and the rain splashed and pattered against the windows. This strange, wild story seemed to have come to us from amid the mad elements – blown in upon us like a sheet of sea-weed[9] in a gale – and now to have been reabsorbed by them once more.

Sherlock Holmes sat for some time in silence with his head sunk forward, and his eyes bent upon the red glow of the fire. Then he lit his pipe, and leaning back in his chair he watched the blue smoke rings as they chased each other up to the ceiling.

'I think, Watson,' he remarked at last, 'that of all our cases we have had none more fantastic than this.'

1. en attendant
2. j'ose espérer
3. ne sauriez être trop prudent
4. le rechercherai
5. viendrai vous voir
6. suivrai vos conseils
7. en tous points
8. prit congé
9. algues

'Save, perhaps, *the Sign of Four*[1].'

'Well, yes. Save, perhaps, that. And yet this John Openshaw seems to me to be walking amid even greater perils than did the Sholtos.'

'But have you,' I asked, 'formed any definite[2] conception[3] as to what these perils are?'

'There can be no question as to their nature[4],' he answered.

'Then what are they? Who is this K. K. K., and why does he pursue this unhappy family?'

Sherlock Holmes closed his eyes, and placed his elbows upon the arms of his chair, with his finger-tips together. 'The ideal reasoner,' he remarked, 'would, when he has once been shown a single fact in all its bearings[5], deduce from it not only all the chain of events which led up to it[6], but also all the results which would follow from it[7]. As Cuvier could correctly describe a whole animal by the contemplation of a single bone, so the observer who has thoroughly[8] understood one link[9] in a series of incidents, should be able accurately[10] to state[11] all the other ones, both before and after. We have not yet grasped[12] the results which the reason alone can attain to[13]. Problems may be solved in the study[14] which have baffled[15] all those who have sought a solution by the aid of their senses. To carry the art, however, to its highest pitch[16], it is necessary that the reasoner should be able to utilize all the facts which have come to his knowledge[17], and this in itself implies, as you will readily[18] see, a possession of all knowledge, which, even in these days of free education and encyclopædias, is a somewhat rare accomplishment[19]. It is not so impossible, however, that a man should possess all knowledge which is likely to be useful to him[20] in his work, and this I have endeavoured[21] in my case[22] to do. If I remem-

1. *Le Signe des quatre* [roman de 1890]
2. précise
3. idée
4. Leur nature ne laisse place à aucun doute
5. sous tous ses aspects
6. y ont conduit
7. vont probablement en découler
8. parfaitement
9. maillon
10. avec précision
11. de nommer
12. saisi
13. atteindre
14. en chambre
15. laissé perplexes
16. à son plus haut degré
17. connaissance
18. sans peine
19. talent
20. lui sera probablement utile
21. me suis efforcé
22. en ce qui me concerne

ber rightly, you on one occasion, in the early days of our friendship, defined my limits in a very precise fashion[1].'

'Yes,' I answered, laughing. 'It was a singular document. Philosophy, astronomy, and politics were marked at[2] zero, I remember. Botany variable, geology profound[3] as regards the[4] mud-stains from any region within[5] fifty miles of town, chemistry eccentric[6], anatomy unsystematic[7], sensational literature and crime records[8] unique[9], violin player, boxer, swordsman[10], lawyer[11], and self-poisoner[12] by cocaine and tobacco. Those, I think, were the main points of my analysis.'

Holmes grinned[13] at the last item. 'Well,' he said, 'I say now, as I said then, that a man should keep his little brain attic[14] stocked with all the furniture that he is likely to use, and the rest he can put away in the lumber-room[15] of his library[16], where he can get it if he wants it. Now, for such a case as the one which has been submitted to us tonight, we need certainly to muster[17] all our resources. Kindly hand me down[18] the letter K of the American Encyclopædia which stands upon the shelf beside you. Thank you. Now let us consider the situation, and see what may be deduced from it. In the first place, we may start with a strong presumption that Colonel Openshaw had some very strong reason for leaving America. Men at his time of life[19] do not change all their habits[20], and exchange willingly[21] the charming climate of Florida for the lonely life of an English provincial town. His extreme love of solitude in England suggests the idea that he was in fear of someone or something, which drove him from[22] America. As to what it was he feared, we can only deduce that by considering the formidable[23] letters

1. façon
2. ont récolté un
3. Connaissances approfondies
4. quant aux
5. dans un rayon
6. Connaissances originales
7. Connaissances peu systématiques
8. antécédents judiciaires
9. Connaissances exceptionnelles
10. escrimeur
11. criminaliste
12. auto-empoisonneur
13. sourit
14. grenier mental
15. réserve
16. bibliothèque
17. rassembler
18. Passez-moi s'il vous plaît
19. de son âge
20. habitudes
21. de bonne grâce
22. lui a fait quitter
23. redoutables

which were received by himself and his successors. Did you remark the postmarks of those letters?'

'The first was from Pondicherry, the second from Dundee, and the third from London.'

'From East London. What do you deduce from that?'

'They are all sea-ports. That the writer was on board a ship.'

'Excellent. We have already a clue[1]. There can be no doubt that the probability – the strong probability – is that the writer was on board of a ship. And now let us consider another point. In the case of Pondicherry seven weeks elapsed[2] between the threat[3] and its fulfilment[4], in Dundee it was only some three or four days. Does that suggest anything?'

'A greater distance to travel.'

'But the letter had also a greater distance to come.'

'Then I do not see the point[5].'

'There is at least a presumption that the vessel[6] in which the man or men are is a sailing ship[7]. It looks as if[8] they always sent their singular warning[9] or token[10] before them when starting upon their mission. You see how quickly the deed[11] followed the sign when it came from Dundee. If they had come from Pondicherry in a steamer they would have arrived almost as soon as their letter. But as a matter of fact seven weeks elapsed. I think that those seven weeks represented the difference between the mail boat[12] which brought the letter, and the sailing vessel which brought the writer.'

'It is possible.'

'More than that. It is probable. And now you see the deadly[13] urgency of this new case, and why I urged[14] young Openshaw to caution[15]. The blow

1. indice
2. se sont écoulées
3. la menace
4. son exécution
5. le rapport
6. navire
7. soit un bateau à voiles
8. Il semblerait qu'
9. avertissement
10. signe
11. forfait
12. navire postal
13. cruciale
14. j'ai exhorté
15. à prendre garde

has always fallen at the end of the time which it would take the senders[1] to travel[2] the distance. But this one comes from London, and therefore we cannot count upon delay.'

'Good God!' I cried. 'What can it mean, this relentless[3] persecution?'

'The papers which Openshaw carried are obviously of vital importance to the person or persons in the sailing ship. I think that it is quite clear that there must be more than one of them. A single man could not have carried out two deaths[4] in such a way as to deceive[5] a coroner's jury. There must have been several in it, and they must have been men of resource and determination. Their papers they mean to have[6], be the holder of them who it may[7]. In this way you see K. K. K. ceases to be the initials of an individual, and becomes the badge[8] of a society.'

'But of what society?'

'Have you never–' said Sherlock Holmes, bending forward[9] and sinking his voice[10] – 'have you never heard of the Ku Klux Klan?'

'I never have.'

Holmes turned over the leaves of the book upon his knee. 'Here it is,' said he presently, "Ku Klux Klan. A name derived from a fanciful[11] resemblance to the sound produced by cocking a rifle[12]. This terrible secret society was formed by some ex-Confederate soldiers in the Southern States after the Civil War[13], and it rapidly formed local branches in different parts of the country, notably in Tennessee, Louisiana, the Carolinas, Georgia, and Florida. Its power was used for political purposes[14], principally for the terrorizing of the negro voters[15], and the murdering or driving from the country of[16] those who were opposed to its views.

1. expéditeurs
2. parcourir
3. implacable
4. commettre deux meurtres
5. d'une façon qui abuse
6. Ils sont décidés à récupérer leurs documents
7. quel que soit leur détenteur
8. le sigle
9. en avant
10. baissant la voix
11. imaginaire
12. l'armement d'un fusil
13. guerre de Sécession
14. à des fins politiques
15. terroriser les électeurs noirs
16. assassiner ou faire fuir

Its outrages[1] were usually preceded by a warning sent to the marked[2] man in some fantastic but generally recognized[3] shape – a sprig[4] of oak leaves in some parts, melon seeds[5] or orange pips in others. On receiving this the victim might either openly abjure his former ways[6], or might fly from the country. If he braved the matter out[7], death would unfailingly come upon him, and usually in some strange and unforeseen[8] manner. So perfect was the organization of the society, and so systematic its methods, that there is hardly a case upon record[9] where any man succeeded[10] in braving it with impunity, or in which any of its outrages were traced home to the perpetrators[11]. For some years the organization flourished[12], in spite of the efforts of the United States Government, and of the better classes of the community in the South[13]. Eventually[14], in the year 1869, the movement rather suddenly collapsed[15], although there have been sporadic outbreaks of the same sort[16] since that date."

'You will observe,' said Holmes, laying down the volume, 'that the sudden breaking up of the society was coincident with the disappearance of Openshaw from America with their papers. It may well have been cause and effect. It is no wonder[17] that he and his family have some of the more implacable spirits upon their track. You can understand that this register and diary may implicate some of the first[18] men in the South, and that there may be many who will not sleep easy at night until it is recovered.'

'Then the page which we have seen–'

'Is such as we might expect. It ran[19], if I remember right, "sent the pips to A, B, and C" – that is, sent the society's warning to them. Then there are successive entries[20] that A and B cleared[21], or left

1. exactions
2. visé
3. reconnaissable
4. brindille
5. des graines
6. renoncer à sa vie d'avant
7. résistait
8. inattendue
9. on ne connaît pour ainsi dire aucun cas
10. quelqu'un ait réussi
11. où l'on ait pu identifier les coupables
12. a prospéré
13. la société sudiste
14. Finalement
15. s'est effondré
16. des résurgences
17. Il n'est pas étonnant
18. les plus éminents
19. disait
20. une série de notes mentionnant
21. ont disparu [ou sont blanchis]

the country, and finally that C was visited, with, I fear, a sinister result for C. Well, I think, Doctor, that we may let some light into this dark place, and I believe that the only[1] chance young Openshaw has in the meantime[2] is to do what I have told him. There is nothing more to be said or to be done to-night, so hand me over[3] my violin and let us try to forget for half an hour the miserable weather, and the still more miserable ways of our fellow-men[4].'

It had cleared in the morning, and the sun was shining with a subdued brightness[5] through the dim veil which hangs over the great city. Sherlock Holmes was already at breakfast when I came down.

'You will excuse me for not waiting for you,' said he; 'I have, I foresee[6], a very busy day before me in looking into this case of young Openshaw's.'

'What steps will you take?' I asked.

'It will very much depend upon the results of my first inquiries. I may have to go down to Horsham after all.'

'You will not go there first?'

'No, I shall commence with the City. Just ring the bell, and the maid will bring up your coffee.

As I waited, I lifted the unopened newspaper from the table and glanced my eye over it. It rested upon a heading[7] which sent a chill to my heart[8].

'Holmes,' I cried, 'you are too late.'

'Ah!' said he, laying down his cup, 'I feared as much[9]. How was it done?' He spoke calmly, but I could see that he was deeply moved[10].

'My eye caught the name of Openshaw, and the heading "Tragedy near Waterloo Bridge". Here is the account[11]: "Between nine and ten last night Police Constable[12] Cook, of the H Division, on duty[13] near Waterloo Bridge, heard a cry for help and a

1. seule
2. dans l'intervalle
3. donnez-moi
4. semblables
5. éclat affaibli
6. le prévois
7. titre
8. me glaça le cœur
9. C'est ce que je craignais
10. ému
11. compte rendu
12. l'agent de police
13. en service

splash[1] in the water. The night, however, was extremely dark and stormy, so that, in spite of the help of several passers-by[2], it was quite impossible to effect a rescue. The alarm, however, was given, and by the aid of the water[3] police, the body was eventually recovered[4]. It proved to be that of a young gentleman whose name, as it appears from an envelope which was found in his pocket, was John Openshaw, and whose residence is near Horsham. It is conjectured that he may have been hurrying down to catch the last train from Waterloo station, and that in his haste and the extreme darkness, he missed his path[5] and walked over the edge of one of the small landing-places[6] for river steamboats. The body exhibited no traces of violence, and there can be no doubt that the deceased[7] had been the victim of an unfortunate accident, which should have the effect of calling the attention of the authorities to the condition of the riverside landing-stages[8].''

We sat in silence for some minutes, Holmes more depressed and shaken than I had ever seen him.

'That hurts my pride[9], Watson,' he said at last. 'It is a petty[10] feeling, no doubt, but it hurts my pride. It becomes a personal matter with me now, and, if God sends me health, I shall set my hand upon this gang. That he should come to me for help[11], and that I should send him away to his death–!' He sprang from his chair, and paced about[12] the room – in uncontrollable agitation, with a flush upon his sallow[13] cheeks, and a nervous clasping and unclasping of his long, thin hands.

'They must be cunning devils[14],' he exclaimed at last. 'How could they have decoyed him[15] down there? The Embankment is not on the direct line[16] to the station. The bridge, no doubt, was too crowded, even on such a night, for their purpose[17]. Well,

1. bruit de chute
2. passants
3. fluviale
4. finalement récupéré
5. s'est trompé de chemin
6. débarcadères
7. défunt
8. appontements
9. Je suis blessé dans mon orgueil
10. mesquin
11. Dire qu'il vient solliciter mon aide
12. se mit à arpenter
13. cireuses
14. diablement rusés
15. l'attirer
16. [de métro]
17. exécuter leur dessein

Watson, we shall see who will win in the long run. I am going out now!'

'To the police?'

'No; I shall be my own police. When I have spun the web[1] they may take the flies, but not before.'

All day I was engaged in[2] my professional work, and it was late in the evening before I returned to Baker Street. Sherlock Holmes had not come back yet. It was nearly ten o'clock before he entered, looking pale and worn. He walked up to the side-board[3], and, tearing a piece from the loaf[4], he devoured it voraciously, washing it down with[5] a long draught[6] of water.

'You are hungry,' I remarked.

'Starving. It had escaped my memory. I have had nothing since breakfast.'

'Nothing?'

'Not a bite[7]. I had no time to think of it.'

'And how have you succeeded?'

'Well.'

'You have a clue?'

'I have them in the hollow of my hand[8]. Young Openshaw shall not remain long unavenged[9]. Why[10], Watson, let us put their own devilish trade-mark upon them[11]. It is well thought of!'

'What do you mean?'

He took an orange from the cupboard, and tearing it to pieces, he squeezed out the pips upon the table. Of these he took five, and thrust them into an envelope. On the inside of the flap he wrote, 'S.H. for J.C.' Then he sealed it and addressed it to 'Captain James Calhoun, Barque *Lone Star*, Savannah, Georgia.'

'That will await him when he enters port,' said he, chuckling[12]. 'It may give him a sleepless[13] night.

1. j'aurai tissé la toile,
2. accaparé par
3. buffet
4. miche de pain
5. l'accompagnant d'
6. gorgée
7. bouchée
8. à ma merci
9. sans être vengé
10. Allons
11. prenons-les à leur propre jeu démoniaque
12. avec un petit rire
13. blanche

He will find it as sure a precursor of his fate[1] as Openshaw did before him.'

'And who is this Captain Calhoun?'

'The leader of the gang. I shall have the others, but he first.'

'How did you trace it[2], then?'

He took a large sheet of paper from his pocket, all covered with dates and names.

'I have spent the whole day,' said he, 'over Lloyd's registers[3] and the files of old papers[4], following the future career of every vessel which touched at Pondicherry in January and in February in '83[5]. There were thirty-six ships of fair[6] tonnage which were reported there during those months. Of these, one, the *Lone Star*, instantly attracted my attention, since, although it was reported as having cleared from[7] London, the name is that which is given to one of the States of the Union.'

'Texas, I think.'

'I was not and am not sure which; but I knew that the ship must have an American origin.'

'What then?'

'I searched the Dundee records, and when I found that the barque *Lone Star* was there in January, '85, my suspicion became a certainty. I then inquired as to vessels which lay at present in the port of London.'

'Yes?'

'The *Lone Star* had arrived here last week. I went down to the Albert Dock, and found that she[8] had been taken down the river by the early tide[9] this morning, homeward bound[10] to Savannah. I wired[11] to Gravesend, and learned that she had passed some time ago, and as the wind is easterly[12], I have no doubt that she is now past the Goodwins[13], and not very far from the Isle of Wight.'

1. un aussi sûr présage du sort qui lui est réservé

2. avez-vous remonté leur piste

3. annuaires de navires marchands

4. journaux

5. à retracer, pour tous les navires ayant rallié Pondichéry en janvier et février 83, les itinéraires postérieurs à leur escale

6. bon

7. parti de

8. ce navire

9. marée

10. faisant cap

11. ai télégraphié

12. souffle de l'est

13. [banc de sable près de la côte du Kent]

'What will you do, then?'

'Oh, I have my hand upon him[1]. He and the two mates[2] are, as I learn, the only native-born[3] Americans in the ship. The others are Finns[4] and Germans. I know also that they were all three away from the ship last night. I had it from the stevedore[5], who has been loading their cargo. By the time their sailing ship reaches Savannah the mail-boat will have carried this letter, and the cable will have informed the police of Savannah that these three gentlemen are badly wanted here upon a charge[6] of murder.'

There is ever a flaw[7], however, in the best laid of human plans, and the murderers of John Openshaw were never to receive the orange pips which would show them that another, as cunning[8] and resolute as themselves, was upon their track. Very long and severe were the equinoctial gales[9] of that year. We waited long for news of the *Lone Star* of Savannah, but none ever reached us. We did at last hear that somewhere far out in the Atlantic a shattered sternpost[10] of a boat was seen swinging in the trough[11] of a wave, with the letters 'L. S.' carved[12] upon it, and that is all which we shall ever know of the fate[13] of the *Lone Star*.

1. je le tiens
2. lieutenants
3. de souche
4. des Finlandais
5. docker
6. étant accusés
7. faille
8. rusé
9. tempêtes d'équinoxe
10. l'étambot brisé
11. creux
12. gravées
13. ce qu'il advint

Silver Blaze[1]

1. Flamme

L'énigme que doit résoudre Sherlock Holmes nous plonge dans le milieu des courses hippiques. Les paris sont élevés et les écuries ont beaucoup à perdre.

Certains sont visiblement prêts à faire disparaître le favori de la Wessex Cup de mardi prochain.

'I AM AFRAID, Watson, that I shall have to go,' said Holmes, as we sat down together to our breakfast one morning.

'Go! Where to?'

'To Dartmoor – to King's Pyland.'

I was not surprised. Indeed, my only wonder was[1] that he had not already been mixed up in this extraordinary case, which was the one topic[2] of conversation through the length and breadth of[3] England. For a whole day my companion had rambled[4] about the room with his chin upon his chest and his brows knitted[5], charging and re-charging his pipe with the strongest black tobacco, and absolutely deaf[6] to any of my questions or remarks. Fresh editions of every paper had been sent up by our newsagent[7] only to be glanced over and tossed down[8] into a corner. Yet, silent as he was, I knew perfectly well what it was over which he was brooding[9]. There was but one[10] problem before the public which could challenge[11] his powers of analysis, and that was the singular disappearance of the favourite for the Wessex Cup, and the tragic murder of its trainer[12]. When, therefore, he suddenly announced his intention of setting out for the scene of the drama, it was only what I had both expected and hoped for.

'I should be most happy to go down with you if I should not be in the way[13],' said I.

'My dear Watson, you would confer[14] a great favour upon me by coming. And I think that your time will not be misspent[15], for[16] there are points about this case which promise to make it an absolutely unique one.

1. je m'étonnais seulement
2. seul sujet
3. à travers toute l'
4. déambulé
5. les sourcils froncés
6. sourd
7. marchand de journaux
8. mais il n'y jetait qu'un coup d'œil avant de les envoyer
9. à quel propos il ruminait
10. Il n'y avait qu'un seul
11. mettre au défi
12. entraîneur
13. ne dérange pas
14. me feriez
15. perdu
16. car

We have, I think, just time to catch our train at Paddington, and I will go further into the matter upon our journey. You would oblige me by bringing with you your very excellent field-glass[1].'

And so it happened that an hour or so later I found myself in the corner of a first-class carriage[2], flying along[3], en route for Exeter, while Sherlock Holmes, with his sharp, eager[4] face framed in his ear-flapped[5] travelling-cap, dipped[6] rapidly into the bundle[7] of fresh papers which he had procured at Paddington. We had left Reading far behind us before he thrust the last of them under the seat, and offered me his cigar-case.

'We are going well,' said he, looking out of the window, and glancing at his watch. 'Our rate[8] at present is fifty-three and a half miles an hour.'

'I have not observed the quarter-mile posts[9],' said I.

'Nor have I. But the telegraph posts upon this line are sixty yards apart, and the calculation is a simple one. I presume that you have already looked into this matter of the murder of John Straker and the disappearance of Silver Blaze?'

'I have seen what the *Telegraph* and the *Chronicle* have to say.'

'It is one of those cases where the art of the reasoner should be used rather for the sifting of[10] details than for the acquiring of[11] fresh evidence[12]. The tragedy has been so uncommon, so complete, and of such personal importance to so many people that we are suffering from a plethora of surmise[13], conjecture, and hypothesis. The difficulty is to detach the framework of fact – of absolute, undeniable fact – from the embellishments[14] of theorists and reporters. Then, having established ourselves upon this sound[15] basis, it is our duty to see what

1. jumelles
2. voiture
3. filant à toute allure
4. vif et ardent
5. à oreillettes
6. se plongeait
7. paquet
8. vitesse
9. poteaux indiquant les quarts de mile
10. plutôt à passer au crible les
11. qu'à trouver
12. de nouveaux indices
13. suppositions
14. fioritures
15. solide

inferences[1] may be drawn, and which are the special points upon which the whole mystery turns. On Tuesday evening I received telegrams, both from Colonel Ross, the owner of the horse, and from Inspector Gregory, who is looking after the case[2], inviting my cooperation.'

'Tuesday evening!' I exclaimed. 'And this is Thursday morning. Why did you not go down yesterday?'

'Because I made a blunder[3], my dear Watson – which is, I am afraid, a more common occurrence than anyone would think who only knew me through your memoirs. The fact is that I could not believe it possible that the most remarkable horse in England could long remain concealed, especially in so sparsely inhabited a place as[4] the north of Dartmoor. From hour to hour yesterday I expected to hear that he had been found, and that his abductor[5] was the murderer of John Straker. When, however, another morning had come and I found that, beyond[6] the arrest of young Fitzroy Simpson, nothing had been done, I felt that it was time for me to take action. Yet in some ways I feel that yesterday has not been wasted[7].'

'You have formed a theory then?'

'At least I have a grip of[8] the essential facts of the case. I shall enumerate them to you, for nothing clears up a case so much as stating it[9] to another person, and I can hardly expect[10] your cooperation if I do not show you the position from which we start.'

I lay back against the cushions, puffing at[11] my cigar, while Holmes, leaning forward, with his long thin forefinger checking off[12] the points upon the palm of his left hand, gave me a sketch[13] of the events which had led to our journey[14].

1. conclusions
2. chargé de l'affaire
3. bourde
4. une région aussi faiblement peuplée que
5. ravisseur
6. à part
7. perdu
8. saisis
9. que de l'exposer
10. ne puis guère escompter
11. en tirant sur
12. décomptant
13. description
14. voyage

'Silver Blaze,' said he, 'is from the Isonomy stock[1], and holds as brilliant a record[2] as his famous ancestor. He is now in his fifth year, and has brought in turn each of the prizes of the turf[3] to Colonel Ross, his fortunate owner[4]. Up to the time[5] of the catastrophe he was first favourite for the Wessex Cup, the betting[6] being three to one on[7]. He has always, however, been a prime favourite with the racing public, and has never yet disappointed them, so that even at short odds[8] enormous sums of money have been laid upon him. It is obvious, therefore, that there were many people who had the strongest interest in preventing[9] Silver Blaze from being there at the fall of the flag[10] next Tuesday.

'This fact was, of course, appreciated[11] at King's Pyland, where the Colonel's training stable[12] is situated. Every precaution was taken to guard the favourite. The trainer, John Straker, is a retired[13] jockey, who rode in Colonel Ross's colours before he became too heavy for the weighing-chair[14]. He has served the Colonel for five years as jockey, and for seven as trainer, and has always shown himself to be a zealous[15] and honest servant. Under him[16] were three lads, for the establishment was a small one, containing only four horses in all. One of these lads sat up[17] each night in the stable[18], while the others slept in the loft[19]. All three bore[20] excellent characters[21]. John Straker, who is a married man, lived in a small villa about two hundred yards from the stables. He has no children, keeps one maid-servant, and is comfortably off[22]. The country round[23] is very lonely[24], but about half a mile to the north there is a small cluster[25] of villas which have been built by a Tavistock contractor[26] for the use of invalids and others who may wish to enjoy the pure Dartmoor air. Tavistock itself lies two miles to

1. de la lignée d'Isonomy
2. palmarès
3. des courses hippiques
4. heureux propriétaire
5. Jusqu'au moment
6. la cote
7. en sa faveur
8. faible cote
9. à empêcher
10. au départ de la course
11. pris en compte
12. écuries d'entraînement
13. ancien
14. la balance
15. zélé
16. Sous ses ordres
17. veillait
18. écurie
19. grenier
20. possédaient
21. références
22. vit dans l'aisance
23. alentour
24. peu peuplée
25. groupe
26. entrepreneur

the west, while across the moor[1], also about two miles distant, is the larger training establishment of Capleton, which belongs to Lord Backwater, and is managed by Silas Brown. In every other direction the moor is a complete wilderness[2], inhabited only by a few roaming[3] gipsies[4]. Such was the general situation last Monday night, when the catastrophe occurred.

'On that evening the horses had been exercised and watered[5] as usual, and the stables were locked up at nine o'clock. Two of the lads walked up to the trainer's house, where they had supper in the kitchen, while the third, Ned Hunter, remained on guard. At a few minutes after nine the maid, Edith Baxter, carried down to the stables his supper, which consisted of a dish of curried mutton[6]. She took no liquid, as there was a water-tap[7] in the stables, and it was the rule that the lad on duty should drink nothing else. The maid carried a lantern with her, as it was very dark, and the path ran across the open moor.

'Edith Baxter was within thirty yards of the stables when a man appeared out of the darkness and called to her to stop. As he stepped[8] into the circle of yellow light thrown by the lantern she saw that he was a person of gentlemanly bearing[9], dressed in a grey suit of tweed with a cloth cap. He wore gaiters[10], and carried a heavy stick with a knob[11] to it. She was most impressed, however, by the extreme pallor of his face and by the nervousness of his manner. His age, she thought, would be rather over thirty than under it.

' "Can you tell me where I am?" he asked. "I had almost made up my mind to[12] sleep on the moor when I saw the light of your lantern."

1. lande
2. totalement désertique
3. itinérants
4. bohémiens
5. on avait fait travailler les chevaux et on leur avait donné à boire
6. mouton au curry
7. robinet
8. s'avançait
9. ayant le maintien d'un gentleman
10. des guêtres
11. pommeau
12. m'étais presque décidé à

1. près
2. chance
3. crois savoir
4. gagner
5. gilet
6. Veille à ce que
7. robe
8. gravité
9. l'inconnu
10. dépassant
11. Qu'avez-vous à faire
12. Des affaires
13. inscrits dans
14. bon tuyau
15. Est-il vrai
16. selon le handicap [le poids supplémentaire]
17. prendre une centaine de mètres d'avance sur l'autre
18. en un kilomètre
19. sales revendeurs [d'informations permettant de parier gagnant]
20. détacher

' "You are close[1] to the King's Pyland training stables," she said.

' "Oh, indeed! What a stroke of luck[2]!" he cried. "I understand[3] that a stable boy sleeps there alone every night. Perhaps that is his supper which you are carrying to him. Now I am sure that you would not be too proud to earn[4] the price of a new dress, would you?" He took a piece of white paper folded up out of his waistcoat[5] pocket. "See that[6] the boy has this tonight, and you shall have the prettiest frock[7] that money can buy."

'She was frightened by the earnestness[8] of his manner, and ran past him to the window through which she was accustomed to hand the meals. It was already open, and Hunter was seated at the small table inside. She had begun to tell him of what had happened, when the stranger[9] came up again.

' "Good evening," said he, looking through the window, "I wanted to have a word with you." The girl has sworn that as he spoke she noticed the corner of the little paper packet protruding[10] from his closed hand.

' "What business have you[11] here?" asked the lad.

' "It's business[12] that may put something into your pocket," said the other. "You've two horses in for[13] the Wessex Cup – Silver Blaze and Bayard. Let me have the straight tip[14], and you won't be a loser. Is it a fact[15] that at the weights[16] Bayard could give the other a hundred yards[17] in five furlongs[18], and that the stable have put their money on him?"

' "So you're one of those damned touts[19]," cried the lad. "I'll show you how we serve them in King's Pyland." He sprang up and rushed across the stable to unloose[20] the dog. The girl fled away to the house, but as she ran she looked back, and saw that the stranger was leaning through the window. A minute later, however, when Hunter rushed out with the hound[1] he was gone, and though the lad ran all round the buildings he failed to find any trace of him.'

'One moment!' I asked. 'Did the stable boy, when he ran out with the dog, leave the door unlocked behind him?'

'Excellent, Watson; excellent!' murmured my companion. 'The importance of the point struck me so forcibly[2], that I sent a special wire to Dartmoor yesterday to clear the matter up[3]. The boy locked the door before he left it. The window, I may add, was not large enough for a man to get through.

'Hunter waited until his fellow-grooms[4] had returned, when he sent a message up to the trainer and told him what had occurred. Straker was excited at hearing the account[5], although he does not seem to have quite realized its true significance. It left him, however, vaguely uneasy, and Mrs. Straker, waking at one in the morning, found that he was dressing. In reply to her inquiries[6], he said that he could not sleep on account of[7] his anxiety about the horses, and that he intended to walk down to the stables to see that all was well. She begged him to remain at home, as she could hear the rain pattering against[8] the windows, but in spite of her entreaties[9] he pulled on[10] his large mackintosh and left the house.

'Mrs. Straker awoke at seven in the morning, to find that her husband had not yet returned. She dressed herself hastily, called the maid, and set off[11] for the stables. The door was open; inside, huddled together[12] upon a chair, Hunter was sunk in a state of absolute stupor[13], the favourite's stall[14] was empty, and there were no signs of his trainer.

1. chien
2. avec une telle force
3. éclaicir ce point
4. les autres palefreniers
5. ce récit
6. questions
7. en raison de
8. crépiter sur
9. supplications,
10. a enfilé
11. est partie
12. tassé
13. hébétude
14. box

1. grenier où l'on hache la paille
2. sellerie
3. ont tous les deux le sommeil profond
4. rien de sensé
5. des [deux] absents
6. monticule
7. leur signala
8. claquait au vent sur
9. buisson d'ajoncs
10. cuvette naturelle
11. blessé à la cuisse
12. infligée manifestement
13. couvert de sang séché
14. jusqu'au manche
15. agrippait
16. une fois sorti de son hébétude
17. catégorique
18. sur l'identité du propriétaire

'The two lads who slept in the chaff-cutting loft[1] above the harness-room[2] were quickly roused. They had heard nothing during the night, for they are both sound sleepers[3]. Hunter was obviously under the influence of some powerful drug; and, as no sense[4] could be got out of him, he was left to sleep it off while the two lads and the two women ran out in search of the absentees[5]. They still had hopes that the trainer had for some reason taken out the horse for early exercise, but on ascending the knoll[6] near the house, from which all the neighbouring moors were visible, they not only could see no signs of the favourite, but they perceived something which warned them[7] that they were in the presence of a tragedy.

'About a quarter of a mile from the stables, John Straker's overcoat was flapping from[8] a furze bush[9]. Immediately beyond there was a bowl-shaped depression[10] in the moor, and at the bottom of this was found the dead body of the unfortunate trainer. His head had been shattered by a savage blow from some heavy weapon, and he was wounded in the thigh[11], where there was a long, clean cut, inflicted evidently[12] by some very sharp instrument. It was clear, however, that Straker had defended himself vigorously against his assailants, for in his right hand he held a small knife, which was clotted with blood[13] up to the handle[14], while in his left he grasped[15] a red and black silk cravat, which was recognized by the maid as having been worn on the preceding evening by the stranger who had visited the stables.

'Hunter, on recovering from his stupor[16], was also quite positive[17] as to the ownership[18] of the cravat. He was equally certain that the same stranger had, while standing at the window, drugged his curried mutton, and so deprived[1] the stables of their watchman.

'As to the missing horse, there were abundant proofs in the mud which lay at the bottom of the fatal hollow, that he had been there at the time of the struggle. But from that morning he has disappeared; and although a large reward[2] has been offered, and all the gipsies of Dartmoor are on the alert, no news has come of him. Finally an analysis has shown that the remains of his supper, left by the stable lad, contain an appreciable quantity of powdered opium, while the people of the house partook of[3] the same dish on the same night without any ill effect.

'Those are the main facts of the case stripped of all surmise[4] and stated as baldly[5] as possible. I shall now recapitulate what the police have done in the matter.

'Inspector Gregory, to whom the case has been committed[6], is an extremely competent officer. Were he but gifted with[7] imagination he might rise to great heights[8] in his profession. On his arrival he promptly found and arrested the man upon whom suspicion naturally rested. There was little difficulty in finding him, for he was thoroughly[9] well known in the neighbourhood. His name, it appears, was Fitzroy Simpson. He was a man of excellent birth and education, who had squandered[10] a fortune upon the turf[11], and who lived now by doing a little quiet and genteel[12] bookmaking in the sporting clubs of London. An examination of his betting-book[13] shows that bets to the amount of[14] five thousand pounds had been registered by him against the favourite.

'On being arrested he volunteered the statement[15] that he had come down to Dartmoor in the hope of

1. privé
2. récompense
3. ont partagé
4. dépouillés de toute conjecture
5. donnés de façon aussi sobre
6. confiée
7. S'il était doué d'
8. des sommets
9. très
10. dilapidé
11. aux courses [hippiques]
12. respectable
13. carnet de paris
14. à hauteur de
15. il a déclaré spontanément

getting some information about the King's Pyland horses, and also about Desborough, the second favourite, which was in charge of[1] Silas Brown, at the Capleton stables. He did not attempt to deny that he had acted as described upon the evening before, but declared that he had no sinister designs[2], and had simply wished to obtain first-hand information. When confronted with the cravat he turned very pale, and was utterly unable to account for[3] its presence in the hand of the murdered man. His wet clothing showed that he had been out in the storm of the night before, and his stick[4], which was a Penang lawyer[5], weighted with lead[6], was just such a weapon[7] as might, by repeated blows, have inflicted the terrible injuries to which the trainer had succumbed.

'On the other hand, there was no wound[8] upon his person, while[9] the state of Straker's knife would show that one, at least, of his assailants must bear his mark upon him. There you have it all in a nutshell[10], Watson, and if you can give me any light I shall be infinitely obliged to you.'

I had listened with the greatest interest to the statement which Holmes, with characteristic clearness, had laid before me. Though most of the facts were familiar to me, I had not sufficiently appreciated their relative importance, nor their connection with each other.

'Is it not possible,' I suggested, 'that the incised wound[11] upon Straker may have been caused by his own knife in the convulsive struggles[12] which follow any brain injury?'

'It is more than possible; it is probable,' said Holmes. 'In that case, one of the main points in favour of the accused disappears.'

1. sous la responsabilité de
2. mauvaises intentions
3. incapable d'expliquer
4. canne
5. « juge de paix malais » [canne façonnée dans une tige de palmier du S.-E. asiatique]
6. lestée de plomb
7. tout à fait le type d'arme
8. blessure
9. alors que
10. Voici l'affaire résumée en quelques mots
11. entaille
12. convulsions

'And yet,' said I, 'even now I fail to understand what the theory of the police can be.'

'I am afraid that whatever theory we state has very grave objections to it,' returned my companion. 'The police imagine, I take it[1], that this Fitzroy Simpson, having drugged the lad, and having in some way obtained a duplicate key[2], opened the stable door, and took out the horse, with the intention, apparently, of kidnapping him altogether. His bridle[3] is missing, so that Simpson must have put it on. Then, having left the door open behind him, he was leading the horse away over the moor, when he was either met or overtaken[4] by the trainer. A row[5] naturally ensued[6], Simpson beat out[7] the trainer's brains[8] with his heavy stick without receiving any injury from the small knife which Straker used in self-defence, and then the thief either led the horse on to some secret hiding-place, or else it may have bolted[9] during the struggle, and be now wandering out[10] on the moors. That is the case as it appears to the police, and improbable as it is[11], all other explanations are more improbable still. However, I shall very quickly test the matter when I am once upon the spot[12], and until then I really cannot see how we can get much further than our present position.'

It was evening before we reached the little town of Tavistock, which lies, like the boss of a shield[13], in the middle of the huge circle of Dartmoor. Two gentlemen were awaiting us at the station; the one[14] a tall fair man with lion-like hair and beard, and curiously penetrating light blue eyes, the other a small alert person, very neat[15] and dapper[16], in a frock-coat[17] and gaiters, with trim[18] little side-whiskers[19] and an eyeglass[20]. The latter was Colonel Ross, the well-known sportsman, the other

1. crois
2. double de la clé
3. filet
4. rattrapé
5. altercation
6. s'est ensuivie
7. a défoncé
8. la cervelle
9. peut-être s'est-il échappé
10. erre-t-il
11. aussi improbable qu'elle soit
12. serai sur place
13. la partie bombée d'un bouclier
14. premier
15. soigné
16. élégant
17. redingote
18. bien taillés
19. favoris
20. monocle

Inspector Gregory, a man who was rapidly making his name in the English detective service.

'I am delighted that you have come down, Mr. Holmes,' said the Colonel. 'The Inspector here has done all that could possibly be suggested[1]; but I wish to leave no stone unturned[2] in trying to avenge[3] poor Straker, and in recovering[4] my horse.'

'Have there been any fresh developments?' asked Holmes.

'I am sorry to say that we have made very little progress,' said the Inspector. 'We have an open carriage[5] outside, and as you would no doubt like to see the place before the light fails, we might talk it over as we drive.'

A minute later we were all seated in a comfortable landau and were rattling through[6] the quaint[7] old Devonshire town. Inspector Gregory was full of his case, and poured out[8] a stream of remarks, while Holmes threw in an occasional question or interjection. Colonel Ross leaned back with his arms folded[9] and his hat tilted[10] over his eyes, while I listened with interest to the dialogue of the two detectives. Gregory was formulating his theory, which was almost exactly what Holmes had foretold[11] in the train.

'The net is drawn[12] pretty close[13] round Fitzroy Simpson,' he remarked, 'and I believe myself that he is our man. At the same time, I recognize that the evidence is purely circumstantial[14], and that some new development may upset it[15].'

'How about Straker's knife?'

'We have quite come to the conclusion that he wounded himself in his fall.'

'My friend Dr. Watson made that suggestion to me as we came down. If so, it would tell against[16] this man Simpson.'

1. envisagé
2. ne veux ménager aucun effort
3. venger
4. retrouver
5. voiture découverte
6. traversions dans un bruit de ferraille
7. pittoresque
8. déversait
9. croisés
10. incliné
11. conjecturé
12. se resserre
13. assez étroitement
14. preuves ne sont qu'indirectes
15. les remettre en cause
16. cela plaiderait contre

'Undoubtedly. He has neither a knife nor any sign of a wound. The evidence[1] against him is certainly very strong. He had a great interest in the disappearance of the favourite, he lies under the suspicion[2] of having poisoned the stable boy, he was undoubtedly out in the storm, he was armed with a heavy stick, and his cravat was found in the dead man's hand. I really think we have enough to go before a jury.'

Holmes shook his head. 'A clever counsel[3] would tear it all to rags[4],' said he. 'Why should he take the horse out of the stable? If he wished to injure it, why could he not do it there? Has a duplicate key been found in his possession? What chemist[5] sold him the powdered opium? Above all, where could he, a stranger to the district, hide a horse, and such a horse as this? What is his own explanation as to the paper which he wished the maid to give to the stable boy?'

'He says that it was a ten-pound note[6]. One was found in his purse[7]. But your other difficulties are not so formidable[8] as they seem. He is not a stranger to the district. He has twice lodged at Tavistock in the summer. The opium was probably brought from London. The key, having served its purpose[9], would be hurled away[10]. The horse may lie at the bottom of one of the pits[11] or old mines upon the moor.'

'What does he say about the cravat?'

'He acknowledges[12] that it is his, and declares that he had lost it. But a new element has been introduced into the case which may account for[13] his leading the horse from[14] the stable.'

Holmes pricked up his ears[15].

'We have found traces which show that a party[16] of gipsies encamped on Monday night within a mile

1. Les preuves
2. on le soupçonne
3. avocat de la défense
4. en ferait de la charpie
5. pharmacien
6. billet de 10 £
7. portefeuille
8. insurmontables
9. ayant rempli son office
10. a dû être jetée au loin
11. carrières [de craie]
12. reconnaît
13. expliquer
14. qu'il ait sorti le cheval de
15. dressa l'oreille
16. groupe

of the spot where the murder took place. On Tuesday they were gone. Now, presuming that there was some understanding[1] between Simpson and these gipsies, might he not have been leading the horse to them when he was overtaken, and may they not have him now?'

'It is certainly possible.'

'The moor is being scoured for[2] these gipsies. I have also examined every stable and outhouse[3] in Tavistock, and for a radius[4] of ten miles.'

'There is another training stable quite close[5], I understand?'

'Yes, and that is a factor which we must certainly not neglect. As Desborough, their horse, was second in the betting, they had an interest in the disappearance of the favourite. Silas Brown, the trainer, is known to have had large bets[6] upon the event, and he was no friend to poor Straker. We have, however, examined the stables, and there is nothing to connect him with the affair.'

'And nothing to connect this man Simpson with the interests of the Capleton stable?'

'Nothing at all.'

Holmes leaned back in the carriage and the conversation ceased. A few minutes later our driver pulled up[7] at a neat[8] little red-brick villa with overhanging eaves[9], which stood by the road. Some distance off, across a paddock[10], lay a long grey-tiled outbuilding[11]. In every other direction the low curves of the moor, bronze-coloured from the fading[12] ferns[13], stretched away to the skyline, broken only by the steeples[14] of Tavistock, and by a cluster of houses away to the westward, which marked the Capleton stables. We all sprang out with the exception of Holmes, who continued to lean back with his eyes fixed upon the sky in front of

1. arrangement
2. On ratisse la lande pour retrouver
3. remise
4. dans un rayon
5. proche
6. pour avoir parié gros
7. s'arrêta
8. jolie
9. des avant-toits
10. à l'autre bout d'un enclos
11. dépendance
12. flétries
13. fougères
14. clochers

him, entirely absorbed in his own thoughts. It was only when I touched his arm that he roused himself with a violent start[1] and stepped out of the carriage.

'Excuse me,' said he, turning to Colonel Ross, who had looked at him in some surprise. 'I was daydreaming[2].' There was a gleam[3] in his eyes and a suppressed[4] excitement in his manner which convinced me, used as I was to his ways[5], that his hand was upon a clue[6], though I could not imagine where he had found it.

'Perhaps you would prefer at once to go on to the scene of the crime, Mr. Holmes?' said Gregory.

'I think that I should prefer to stay here a little and go into[7] one or two questions of detail. Straker was brought back here, I presume?'

'Yes, he lies upstairs. The inquest[8] is tomorrow.'

'He has been in your service some years, Colonel Ross?'

'I have always found him an excellent servant.'

'I presume that you made an inventory[9] of what he had in his pockets at the time of his death, Inspector?'

'I have the things themselves in the sitting-room, if you would care to see them.'

'I should be very glad.'

We all filed[10] into the front room, and sat round the central table, while the Inspector unlocked a square tin[11] box and laid a small heap[12] of things before us. There was a box of vestas[13], two inches of tallow candle[14], an A.D.P. briar-root[15] pipe, a pouch of sealskin[16] with half an ounce of long-cut cavendish[17], a silver watch with a gold chain, five sovereigns in gold, an aluminium pencil-case, a few papers, and an ivory-handled[18] knife with a very delicate inflexible blade[19] marked Weiss & Co., London.

1. sursaut
2. rêvassais
3. lueur
4. contenue
5. sa façon d'être
6. qu'il tenait une piste
7. approfondir
8. audience [du coroner]
9. inventaire
10. entrâmes un à un
11. en fer-blanc
12. tas
13. allumettes
14. chandelle de suif
15. de racine de bruyère, de la marque ADP
16. blague à tabac en peau de phoque
17. une quinzaine de de grammes de tabac en *flakes* [gros copeaux]
18. à manche d'ivoire
19. lame

'This is a very singular knife,' said Holmes, lifting it up and examining it minutely[1]. 'I presume, as I see blood-stains upon it, that it is the one which was found in the dead man's grasp. Watson, this knife is surely in your line.'

'It is what we call a cataract[2] knife,' said I.

'I thought so. A very delicate blade devised[3] for very delicate work. A strange thing for a man to carry with him upon[4] a rough[5] expedition, especially as it would not shut in his pocket.'

'The tip[6] was guarded[7] by a disc of cork[8] which we found beside his body,' said the Inspector. 'His wife tells us that the knife had lain for some days upon the dressing-table, and that he had picked it up as he left the room. It was a poor[9] weapon, but perhaps the best that he could lay his hand on at the moment.'

'Very possible. How about these papers?'

'Three of them are receipted hay-dealers' accounts[10]. One of them is a letter of instructions from Colonel Ross. This other is a milliner's account[11] for thirty-seven pounds fifteen, made out by Madame Lesurier, of Bond Street, to William Darbyshire. Mrs. Straker tells us that Darbyshire was a friend of her husband's, and that occasionally his letters were addressed here.'

'Madame Darbyshire had somewhat expensive tastes,' remarked Holmes, glancing down the account. 'Twenty-two guineas is rather heavy[12] for a single costume. However, there appears to be nothing more to learn, and we may now go down to the scene of the crime.'

As we emerged from the sitting-room a woman who had been waiting in the passage took a step forward and laid her hand upon the Inspector's

1. minutieusement
2. ophtalmique
3. conçue
4. lors d'
5. mouvementée
6. La pointe
7. protégée
8. liège
9. piètre
10. des reçus provenant de négociants en foin
11. la facture d'une modiste
12. un peu excessif

sleeve. Her face was haggard, and thin, and eager[1]; stamped with the print[2] of a recent horror.

'Have you got them? Have you found them?' she panted[3].

'No, Mrs. Straker; but Mr. Holmes, here, has come from London to help us, and we shall do all that is possible.'

'Surely I met you in Plymouth, at a garden-party, some little time ago, Mrs. Straker,' said Holmes.

'No, sir; you are mistaken[4].'

'Dear me[5]; why,[6] I could have sworn to it. You wore a costume of dove-coloured[7] silk with ostrich feather[8] trimming[9].'

'I never had such a dress, sir,' answered the lady.

'Ah; that quite settles it[10],' said Holmes; and, with an apology, he followed the Inspector outside. A short walk across the moor took us to the hollow in which the body had been found. At the brink[11] of it was the furze bush upon which the coat had been hung.

'There was no wind that night, I understand,' said Holmes.

'None; but very heavy rain.'

'In that case the overcoat was not blown against[12] the furze bushes, but placed there.'

'Yes, it was laid across the bush.'

'You fill me with interest. I perceive that the ground has been trampled up a good deal[13]. No doubt many feet have been there since Monday night.'

'A piece of matting[14] has been laid here at the side, and we have all stood upon that.'

'Excellent.'

'In this bag I have one of the boots which Straker wore, one of Fitzroy Simpson's shoes, and a cast horseshoe[15] of Silver Blaze.'

1. fiévreux
2. on y voyait la marque
3. dit-elle, haletante
4. vous trompez
5. Çà alors
6. eh bien
7. gris perle
8. en plumes d'autruche
9. une garniture
10. voilà qui règle la question
11. bord
12. apporté par le vent sur
13. passablement piétiné
14. natte
15. un vieux fer

'My dear Inspector, you surpass yourself!'

Holmes took the bag, and descending into the hollow he pushed the matting into a more central position. Then stretching himself upon his face[1] and leaning his chin upon his hands he made a careful study of the trampled mud in front of him.

'Halloa!' said he, suddenly, 'what's this?'

It was a wax vesta[2], half burned, which was so coated with mud that it looked at first like a little chip[3] of wood.

'I cannot think how I came to overlook it[4],' said the Inspector, with an expression of annoyance[5].

'It was invisible, buried in the mud. I only saw it because I was looking for it.'

'What! You expected to find it?'

'I thought it not unlikely[6].' He took the boots from the bag and compared the impressions of each of them with marks upon the ground. Then he clambered up[7] to the rim[8] of the hollow and crawled about[9] among the ferns and bushes.

'I am afraid that there are no more tracks,' said the Inspector. 'I have examined the ground very carefully for a hundred yards in each direction.'

'Indeed!' said Holmes, rising, 'I should not have the impertinence to do it again after what you say. But I should like to take a little walk over the moors before it grows dark, that I may know my ground tomorrow, and I think that I shall put this horseshoe into my pocket for luck.'

Colonel Ross, who had shown some signs of impatience at my companion's quiet and systematic method of work, glanced at his watch.

'I wish you would come back with me, Inspector,' said he. 'There are several points on which I should like your advice, and especially as to whether we

1. allongé à plat ventre
2. allumette de cire
3. éclat
4. elle a pu m'échapper
5. contrariété
6. vraisemblable
7. se hissa
8. jusqu'au rebord
9. rampa

do not owe it[1] to the public to remove our horse's name from the entries for[2] the Cup.'

'Certainly not,' cried Holmes, with decision[3]; 'I should let the name stand[4].'

The Colonel bowed[5]. 'I am very glad to have had your opinion, sir,' said he. 'You will find us at poor Straker's house when you have finished your walk, and we can drive together into Tavistock.'

He turned back with the Inspector, while Holmes and I walked slowly across the moor. The sun was beginning to sink behind the stables of Capleton, and the long sloping[6] plain in front of us was tinged with gold[7], deepening into rich, ruddy brown[8] where the faded ferns and brambles[9] caught the evening light. But the glories[10] of the landscape were all wasted upon my companion, who was sunk in the deepest thought.

'It's this way, Watson,' he said, at last. 'We may leave the question of who killed John Straker for the instant, and confine ourselves to[11] finding out what has become[12] of the horse. Now, supposing that he broke away during or after the tragedy, where could he have gone to? The horse is a very gregarious creature. If left to himself, his instincts would have been either to return to King's Pyland or go over to Capleton. Why should he run wild[13] upon the moor? He would surely have been seen by now. And why should gipsies kidnap him? These people always clear out[14] when they hear of trouble[15], for they do not wish to be pestered[16] by the police. They could not hope to sell such a horse. They would run a great risk and gain nothing by taking him. Surely that is clear.'

'Where is he, then?'

'I have already said that he must have gone to King's Pyland or to Capleton. He is not at King's

1. quant à la question de savoir si nous ne devons pas
2. de la liste des concurrents de
3. détermination
4. figurer
5. s'inclina
6. en pente
7. teintée d'or
8. un beau brun-rouge
9. ronces
10. splendeurs
11. nous borner à
12. ce qu'il est advenu
13. courir en toute liberté
14. décampent
15. apprennent qu'il y a du grabuge
16. harcelés

Pyland, therefore he is at Capleton. Let us take that as a working[1] hypothesis, and see what it leads us to. This part of the moor, as the Inspector remarked, is very hard and dry. But it falls away[2] towards[3] Capleton, and you can see from here that there is a long hollow over yonder[4], which must have been very wet on Monday night. If our supposition is correct, then the horse must have crossed that, and there is the point where we should look for his tracks.'

We had been walking briskly[5] during this conversation, and a few more minutes brought us to the hollow in question. At Holmes' request[6] I walked down the bank[7] to the right, and he to the left, but I had not taken fifty paces before[8] I heard him give a shout, and saw him waving his hand to me. The track of a horse was plainly outlined[9] in the soft earth in front of him, and the shoe which he took from his pocket exactly fitted[10] the impression[11].

'See the value of imagination,' said Holmes. 'It is the one quality which Gregory lacks[12]. We imagined what might have happened, acted upon the supposition[13], and find ourselves justified[14]. Let us proceed[15].'

We crossed the marshy[16] bottom and passed over a quarter of a mile of dry, hard turf[17]. Again the ground sloped and again we came on the tracks. Then we lost them for half a mile, but only to pick them up once more quite close to[18] Capleton. It was Holmes who saw them first, and he stood pointing[19] with a look of triumph upon his face. A man's track was visible beside the horse's.

'The horse was alone before,' I cried.

'Quite so. It was alone before. Halloa! what is this?' The double track turned sharp off[20] and took the direction of King's Pyland. Holmes whistled,

1. de travail
2. s'abaisse
3. en direction de
4. là-bas
5. d'un bon pas
6. la demande
7. talus
8. fait cinquante pas que
9. apparaissait clairement
10. correspondait parfaitement à
11. l'empreinte
12. fait défaut à Gregory
13. suivant cette hypothèse
14. confortés
15. Continuons
16. marécageux
17. terrain herbeux
18. tout près de
19. les désigna du doigt
20. bifurquait brusquement

and we both followed along after it. His eyes were on the trail, but I happened to look a little to one side, and saw to my surprise the same tracks coming back again in the opposite direction.

'One for you[1], Watson,' said Holmes, when I pointed it out; 'you have saved us[2] a long walk which would have brought us back on our own traces. Let us follow the return track.'

We had not to go far. It ended at the paving[3] of asphalt which led up to the gates of the Capleton stables. As we approached a groom ran out from them.

'We don't want any loiterers about here[4],' said he.

'I only wished to ask a question,' said Holmes, with his finger and thumb in his waistcoat pocket. 'Should I be too early to see your master, Mr. Silas Brown, if I were to call[5] at five o'clock tomorrow morning?'

'Bless you, sir, if anyone is about he will be[6], for he is always the first stirring[7]. But here he is, sir, to answer your questions for himself. No, sir, no; it's as much as my place is worth[8] to let him see me[9] touch your money. Afterwards, if you like.'

As Sherlock Holmes replaced the half-crown which he had drawn from his pocket, a fierce-looking[10] elderly[11] man strode out from the gate with a hunting-crop[12] swinging in his hand.

'What's this, Dawson?' he cried. 'No gossiping[13]! Go about your business[14]! And you – what the devil do you want here?'

'Ten minutes' talk with you, my good sir,' said Holmes, in the sweetest of voices.

'I've no time to talk to every gadabout[15]. We want no strangers here. Be off[16], or you may find a dog at your heels.'

1. Un point pour vous
2. nous avez épargné
3. revêtement
4. Vous n'avez pas à traîner par ici
5. me présentais
6. quelqu'un est debout [alors], c'est bien lui
7. levé
8. ma place qui serait en jeu
9. s'il me voyait
10. menaçant
11. âgé
12. cravache
13. Pas de bavardages
14. Retourne à tes occupations
15. vadrouilleur
16. Allez-vous-en

Holmes leaned forward and whispered something in the trainer's ear. He started[1] violently and flushed to the temples[2].

'It's a lie[3]!' he shouted. 'An infernal lie!'

'Very good! Shall we argue about it[4] here in public, or talk it over in your parlour?'

'Oh, come in if you wish to.'

Holmes smiled. 'I shall not keep you more than a few minutes, Watson,' he said. 'Now, Mr. Brown, I am quite at your disposal.'

It was quite twenty minutes, and the reds had all faded into[5] greys before Holmes and the trainer reappeared. Never have I seen such a change as had been brought about in Silas Brown in that short time. His face was ashy pale[6], beads of perspiration shone upon his brow[7], and his hands shook until the hunting-crop wagged[8] like a branch in the wind. His bullying[9], overbearing[10] manner[11] was all gone too, and he cringed along[12] at my companion's side like a dog with its master.

'Your instructions will be done. It shall be done,' said he.

'There must be no mistake,' said Holmes, looking round at him. The other winced[13] as he read the menace in his eyes.

'Oh, no, there shall be no mistake. It shall be there. Should I change it first or not?'

Holmes thought a little and then burst out laughing. 'No, don't,' said he. 'I shall write to you about it. No tricks now or –[14]'

'Oh, you can trust me, you can trust me!'

'You must see to it[15] on the day[16] as if it were your own.'

'You can rely upon me.'

'Yes, I think I can. Well, you shall hear from me tomorrow.' He turned upon his heel, disregarding[17]

1. sursauta
2. le rouge lui monta aux tempes
3. mensonge
4. Allons-nous en débattre
5. laissé place à
6. d'une pâleur de cendre
7. la sueur perlait sur son front
8. à faire trembler violemment sa cravache
9. intimidante
10. autoritaire
11. attitude
12. avançait docilement
13. tressaillit
14. Mais pas d'entourloupe, sinon...
15. y veiller
16. ce jour-là
17. ignorant

the trembling hand which the other held out to him, and we set off for King's Pyland.

'A more perfect compound[1] of the bully[2], coward[3] and sneak[4] than Master Silas Brown I have seldom met with,' remarked Holmes, as we trudged along[5] together.

'He has the horse, then?'

'He tried to bluster out of it[6], but I described to him so exactly what his actions had been upon that morning, that he is convinced that I was watching him. Of course, you observed the peculiarly square toes in the impressions, and that his own boots exactly corresponded to them. Again, of course, no subordinate would have dared to have done such a thing. I described to him how when, according to his custom[7], he was the first down, he perceived a strange horse wandering over the moor; how he went out to it, and his astonishment at recognizing from the white forehead[8] which has given the favourite its name[9] that chance had put in his power the only[10] horse which could beat the one upon which he had put his money[11]. Then I described how his first impulse had been to lead him back to King's Pyland, and how the devil had shown him how he could hide the horse until the race was over, and how he had led it back and concealed it at Capleton. When I told him every detail he gave it up[12], and thought only of saving his own skin.'

'But his stables had been searched.'

'Oh, an old horse-faker[13] like him has many a dodge[14].'

'But are you not afraid to leave the horse in his power now, since he has every interest in injuring it[15]?'

1. mélange
2. tyran
3. lâche
4. sournois
5. cheminions
6. de s'en sortir en tempêtant
7. comme à son habitude
8. en voyant son chanfrein blanc
9. qui a valu au favori son nom,
10. seul
11. sur lequel il avait misé
12. a craqué
13. maquilleur de chevaux
14. plus d'un tour dans son sac
15. tout intérêt à ne pas le laisser indemne

'My dear fellow, he will guard it as the apple of his eye[1]. He knows that his only hope of mercy[2] is to produce it safe.'

'Colonel Ross did not impress me as a man who would be[3] likely to show much mercy in any case.'

'The matter does not rest with[4] Colonel Ross. I follow my own methods, and tell as much or as little as I choose. That is the advantage of being unofficial. I don't know whether you observed it, Watson, but the Colonel's manner has been just a trifle[5] cavalier to me. I am inclined now to have a little amusement at his expense[6]. Say nothing to him about the horse.'

'Certainly not, without your permission.'

'And, of course, this is all quite a minor case compared with the question of who killed John Straker.'

'And you will devote yourself[7] to that?'

'On the contrary, we both go back to London by the night train.'

I was thunderstruck[8] by my friend's words. We had only been a few hours in Devonshire, and that he should give up[9] an investigation which he had begun so brilliantly was quite incomprehensible to me. Not a word more could I draw from him until we were back at the trainer's house. The Colonel and the Inspector were awaiting us in the parlour.

'My friend and I return to town by the midnight express,' said Holmes. 'We have had a charming little breath[10] of your beautiful Dartmoor air.'

The Inspector opened his eyes, and the Colonel's lips curled in a sneer[11].

'So you despair of arresting the murderer of poor Straker,' said he.

Holmes shrugged his[12] shoulders. 'There are certainly grave difficulties in the way,' said he. 'I have every hope, however, that your horse will start

1. prunelle de ses yeux
2. d'indulgence
3. ne m'a pas paru le genre d'homme
4. ne dépend pas du
5. un tant soit peu
6. à ses dépens
7. vous consacrer
8. abasourdi
9. qu'il abandonne
10. bouffée
11. se retroussèrent en un rictus sarcastique
12. haussa les

upon Tuesday, and I beg that you will have your jockey in readiness[1]. Might I ask for a photograph of Mr. John Straker?'

The Inspector took one from an envelope in his pocket and handed it to him.

'My dear Gregory, you anticipate all my wants. If I might ask you to wait here for an instant, I have a question which I should like to put to[2] the maid.'

'I must say that I am rather disappointed in our London consultant,' said Colonel Ross, bluntly[3], as my friend left the room. 'I do not see that we are any further[4] than when he came.'

'At least, you have his assurance that your horse will run,' said I.

'Yes, I have his assurance,' said the Colonel, with a shrug of his shoulders. 'I should prefer to have the horse.'

I was about to make some reply in defence of my friend, when he entered the room again.

'Now, gentlemen,' said he, 'I am quite ready for Tavistock.'

As we stepped into[5] the carriage one of the stable lads held the door open for us. A sudden idea seemed to occur to[6] Holmes, for he leaned forward and touched the lad upon the sleeve.

'You have a few sheep in the paddock,' he said 'Who attends to them[7]?'

'I do, sir.'

'Have you noticed anything amiss[8] with them of late[9]?'

'Well, sir, not of much account[10]; but three of them have gone lame[11], sir.'

I could see that Holmes was extremely pleased, for he chuckled[12] and rubbed his hands together.

'A long shot[13], Watson; a very long shot[14]!' said he, pinching my arm. 'Gregory, let me recommend to[15]

1. vous demande de tenir votre jockey fin prêt
2. poser à
3. sans ambages
4. ne crois pas que nous soyons plus avancés
5. montions dans
6. venir à l'esprit de
7. s'en occupe
8. qui cloche
9. dernièrement
10. rien de bien important
11. se sont mis à boiter
12. eut un petit rire
13. Les chances étaient minces
14. très minces
15. signaler à

your attention this singular epidemic among the sheep. Drive on[1], coachman!'

Colonel Ross still wore an expression which showed the poor[2] opinion which he had formed of my companion's ability[3], but I saw by the Inspector's face that his attention had been keenly[4] aroused[5].

'You consider that to be important?' he asked.

'Exceedingly so[6].'

'Is there any other point to which you would wish to draw my attention?'

'To the curious incident of the dog in the night-time.'

'The dog did nothing in the night-time.'

'That was the curious incident,' remarked Sherlock Holmes.

Four days later Holmes and I were again in the train bound for[7] Winchester, to see the race for the Wessex Cup. Colonel Ross met us, by appointment[8], outside the station, and we drove in his drag[9] to the course[10] beyond the town. His face was grave and his manner was cold in the extreme.

'I have seen nothing of my horse,' said he.

'I suppose that you would know him when you saw him?' asked Holmes.

The Colonel was very angry. 'I have been on the turf for twenty years, and never was asked such a question as that before,' said he. 'A child would know Silver Blaze with his white forehead and his mottled[11] off foreleg[12].'

'How is the betting[13]?'

'Well, that is the curious part of it. You could have got fifteen to one yesterday, but the price has become shorter and shorter[14], until you can hardly get three to one now.'

1. En route
2. piètre
3. capacités
4. vivement
5. éveillée
6. De la plus grande importance
7. à destination de
8. sur rendez-vous
9. [voiture hippomobile à quatre chevaux]
10. champ de courses
11. tacheté
12. antérieur droit
13. Où en sont les paris
14. la cote a baissé, baissé

'Hum!' said Holmes. 'Somebody knows something, that is clear!'

As the drag drew up in the enclosure[1] near the grandstand[2], I glanced at the card[3] to see the entries[4]. It ran[5]:

Wessex Plate. 50 sovs.[6] each, h ft[7], with 1,000 sovs. added, for four- and five-year olds. Second £300. Third £200. New course[8] (one mile and five furlongs[9]).

1. Mr. Heath Newton's The Negro (red cap[10], cinnamon[11] jacket[12]).
2. Colonel Wardlaw's Pugilist (pink cap, blue and black jacket).
3. Lord Backwater's Desborough (yellow cap and sleeves).
4. Colonel Ross's Silver Blaze (black cap, red jacket).
5. Duke of Balmoral's Iris (yellow and black stripes[13]).
6. Lord Singleford's Rasper (purple cap, black sleeves).

'We scratched[14] our other one[15] and put all hopes on your word[16],' said the Colonel. 'Why, what is that? Silver Blaze favourite?'

'Five to four against Silver Blaze!' roared the ring. 'Five to four against Silver Blaze! Fifteen to five against[17] Desborough! Five to four on the field[18]!'

'There are the numbers up[19],' I cried. 'They are all six there.'

'All six there! Then my horse is running,' cried the Colonel, in great agitation. 'But I don't see him. My colours have not passed.'

'Only five have passed. This must be he.'

As I spoke a powerful bay[20] horse swept out from the weighing enclosure[21] and cantered past us[22], bearing on its back the well-known black and red of the Colonel.

'That's not my horse,' cried the owner. 'That beast has not a white hair upon its body. What is this that you have done, Mr. Holmes?'

1. enclos
2. tribune principale
3. programme
4. chevaux au départ
5. On y lisait
6. 50 £ [=50 sovereigns]
7. dont 25 £ de mise initiale non rendue [half forfeit]
8. parcours
9. 2,6 km
10. toque
11. cannelle
12. casaque
13. rayures
14. avons retiré
15. [horse]
16. parole
17. Cote de 3 contre 1, sur
18. au départ
19. Les numéros s'affichent
20. bai
21. pesage
22. passa devant nous au petit galop

'Well, well, let us see how he gets on[1],' said my friend, imperturbably. For a few minutes he gazed through my field-glass. 'Capital[2]! An excellent start!' he cried suddenly. 'There they are, coming round the curve[3]!'

From our drag we had a superb view as they came up the straight[4]. The six horses were so close together[5] that a carpet could have covered them, but half-way up[6] the yellow of the Capleton stable showed to the front[7]. Before they reached us, however, Desborough's bolt[8] was shot[9], and the Colonel's horse, coming away[10] with a rush[11], passed the post[12] a good six lengths before its rival, the Duke of Balmoral's Iris making a bad third.

'It's my race[13] anyhow[14],' gasped[15] the Colonel, passing his hand over his eyes. 'I confess that I can make neither head nor tail of it[16]. Don't you think that you have kept up your mystery long enough, Mr. Holmes?'

'Certainly, Colonel. You shall know everything.

Let us all go round and have a look at the horse together. Here he is,' he continued, as we made our way into the weighing enclosure where only owners and their friends find admittance[17]. 'You have only to wash his face and his leg in spirits of wine[18] and you will find that he is the same old Silver Blaze as ever.'

'You take my breath away[19]!'

'I found him in the hands of a faker, and took the liberty of running him[20] just as he was sent over.'

'My dear sir, you have done wonders[21]. The horse looks very fit and well[22]. It never went better in its life. I owe you a thousand apologies for having doubted your ability. You have done me a great service by recovering[23] my horse. You would do me a greater still if you could lay your hands on the murderer of John Straker.'

1. se débrouille
2. Épatant
3. ils prennent le virage
4. abordaient la ligne droite
5. formaient un groupe si serré
6. à mi-chemin [de la ligne droite]
7. était en tête
8. l'envolée
9. retombait
10. se détachant
11. à toute vitesse
12. arrivée
13. J'ai gagné
14. en tout cas
15. haleta
16. n'y comprends rien
17. ont le droit d'entrer
18. avec de l'esprit de vin
19. Je n'en reviens pas
20. le faire courir
21. merveille
22. en très bonne forme
23. en retrouvant

'I have done so,' said Holmes, quietly.

The Colonel and I stared at him in amazement. 'You have got him! Where is he, then?'

'He is here.'

'Here! Where?'

'In my company at the present moment.'

The Colonel flushed angrily. 'I quite recognize that I am under obligations to you, Mr. Holmes,' said he, 'but I must regard what you have just said as either a very bad joke or an insult.'

Sherlock Holmes laughed. 'I assure you that I have not associated you with the crime, Colonel,' said he; 'the real murderer is standing immediately behind you!'

He stepped past and laid his hand upon the glossy neck of the thoroughbred[1].

'The horse!' cried both the Colonel and myself.

'Yes, the horse. And it may lessen[2] his guilt[3] if I say that it was done in self-defence, and that John Straker was a man who was entirely unworthy[4] of your confidence[5]. But there goes[6] the bell; and as I stand to[7] win a little on this next race, I shall defer[8] a more lengthy[9] explanation until a more fitting[10] time.'

We had the corner of a Pullman car to ourselves that evening as we whirled back[11] to London, and I fancy that the journey was a short one to Colonel Ross as well as to myself, as we listened to our companion's narrative[12] of the events which had occurred at the Dartmoor training stables upon that Monday night, and the means by which he had unravelled them[13].

'I confess,' said he, 'that any theories which I had formed from the newspaper reports were entirely erroneous. And yet there were indications there[14], had they not been overlaid[15] by other details which

1. pur-sang
2. atténuer
3. culpabilité
4. indigne
5. confiance
6. j'entends
7. puis
8. reporterai
9. détaillée
10. approprié
11. retournions à vive allure
12. récit
13. façon dont il les avait démêlés
14. On eût pu y piocher pourtant des renseignements,
15. s'ils n'avaient été occultés

1. portée
2. coupable
3. les preuves
4. n'étaient absolument pas
5. m'apparut
6. étiez tous descendus
7. me demandais vraiment
8. un indice aussi flagrant
9. maillon
10. S'il était
11. moyen de
12. Il est impossible de supposer que
13. ait dicté le choix du curry
14. trop énorme
15. qu'il avait comme par hasard
16. exactement le soir où
17. Donc
18. car
19. néfastes
20. de trancher
21. compris

concealed their true import[1]. I went to Devonshire with the conviction that Fitzroy Simpson was the true culprit[2], although, of course, I saw that the evidence[3] against him was by no means[4] complete.

'It was while I was in the carriage, just as we reached the trainer's house, that the immense significance of the curried mutton occurred to me[5]. You may remember that I was distrait, and remained sitting after you had all alighted[6]. I was marvelling[7] in my own mind how I could possibly have overlooked so obvious a clue[8].'

'I confess,' said the Colonel, 'that even now I cannot see how it helps us.'

'It was the first link[9] in my chain of reasoning. Powdered opium is by no means tasteless. The flavour is not disagreeable, but it is perceptible. Were it[10] mixed with any ordinary dish, the eater would undoubtedly detect it, and would probably eat no more. A curry was exactly the medium which would[11] disguise this taste. By no possible supposition could[12] this stranger, Fitzroy Simpson, have caused curry to be[13] served in the trainer's family that night, and it is surely too monstrous[14] a coincidence to suppose that he happened to come along with[15] powdered opium upon the very night when[16] a dish happened to be served which would disguise the flavour. That is unthinkable. Therefore[17] Simpson becomes eliminated from the case, and our attention centres upon Straker and his wife, the only two people who could have chosen curried mutton for supper that night. The opium was added after the dish was set aside for the stable boy, for[18] the others had the same for supper with no ill[19] effects. Which of them, then, had access to that dish without the maid seeing them?

'Before deciding[20] that question I had grasped[21] the significance of the silence of the dog, for one true inference[1] invariably suggests others. The Simpson incident had shown me that a dog was kept in the stables, and yet, though someone had been in and had fetched out[2] a horse, he had not barked enough to arouse the two lads in the loft. Obviously the midnight visitor was someone whom the dog knew well.

'I was already convinced, or almost convinced, that John Straker went down to the stables in the dead[3] of the night and took out Silver Blaze. For what purpose[4]? For a dishonest one, obviously, or why should he drug his own stable boy? And yet I was at a loss to know[5] why. There have been cases before now where trainers have made sure of[6] great sums of money by laying[7] against their own horses, through agents, and then prevented them[8] from winning by fraud. Sometimes it is a pulling jockey[9]. Sometimes it is some surer and subtler means[10]. What was it here? I hoped that the contents of his pockets might help me to form a conclusion.

'And they did so. You cannot have forgotten the singular knife which was found in the dead man's hand, a knife which certainly no sane[11] man would choose for a weapon. It was, as Dr. Watson told us, a form of knife which is used for the most delicate operations known in surgery[12]. And it was to be used for a delicate operation that night. You must know, with your wide experience of turf matters, Colonel Ross, that it is possible to make a slight nick[13] upon the tendons of a horse's ham[14], and to do it subcutaneously[15] so as to leave[16] absolutely no trace. A horse so treated would develop a slight lameness[17] which would be put down to[18] a strain[19] in exercise or a touch of rheumatism, but never to foul play[20].'

'Villain[21]! Scoundrel[22]!' cried the Colonel.

1. déduction juste
2. fait sortir
3. au cœur
4. Dans quel but
5. ne m'expliquais pas
6. ont empoché
7. en pariant
8. les ont empêchés
9. un jockey qui retient sa monture
10. procédé
11. sain d'esprit
12. en chirurgie
13. entaille
14. jarret
15. sous la peau
16. de façon à ne laisser
17. boiterie
18. mise sur le compte d'
19. effort excessif
20. d'origine criminelle
21. Scélérat
22. Crapule

'We have here the explanation of why John Straker wished to take the horse out on to the moor. So spirited[1] a creature would have certainly roused the soundest of sleepers[2] when it felt the prick[3] of the knife. It was absolutely necessary to do it in the open air.'

'I have been blind!' cried the Colonel. 'Of course, that was why he needed the candle, and struck the match[4].'

'Undoubtedly. But in examining his belongings[5], I was fortunate enough[6] to discover, not only the method of the crime, but even its motives. As a man of the world, Colonel, you know that men do not carry other people's bills[7] about in their pockets. We have most of us quite enough to do to settle our own[8]. I at once concluded that Straker was leading a double life, and keeping a second establishment[9]. The nature of the bill showed that there was a lady in the case, and one who had expensive tastes. Liberal as you are[10] with your servants, one hardly expects that they can buy twenty-guinea walking dresses[11] for their women. I questioned Mrs. Straker as to the dress without her knowing it, and having satisfied myself[12] that it had never reached her, I made a note of the milliner's[13] address, and felt that by calling there[14] with Straker's photograph, I could easily dispose of[15] the mythical Darbyshire.

'From that time on[16] all was plain. Straker had led out the horse to a hollow where his light would be invisible. Simpson, in his flight, had dropped his cravat, and Straker had picked it up with some idea, perhaps, that he might use it in securing[17] the horse's leg. Once in the hollow he had got behind the horse, and had struck a light, but the creature[18], frightened at the sudden glare[19], and with the strange instinct of animals feeling that

1. fougueuse
2. meilleur des dormeurs
3. morsure
4. gratté l'allumette
5. affaires
6. ai eu la chance
7. les factures d'un autre
8. assez à faire avec les nôtres
9. ménage
10. Si généreux que vous soyez
11. toilettes de promenade
12. m'étant assuré
13. de la modiste
14. en me présentant chez elle
15. me débarrasserais facilement
16. Dès lors,
17. pour attacher
18. animal
19. par l'éclat

some mischief[1] was intended[2], had lashed out[3], and the steel shoe[4] had struck Straker full on the forehead. He had already, in spite of the rain, taken off his overcoat in order to do his delicate task, and so, as he fell, his knife gashed[5] his thigh. Do I make it clear?'

'Wonderful!' cried the Colonel. 'Wonderful! You might have been there.'

'My final shot was, I confess, a very long one[6]. It struck me that so astute a man as Straker would not undertake this delicate tendon-nicking without a little practice. What could he practise on[7]? My eyes fell upon the sheep, and I asked a question which, rather to my surprise, showed that my surmise[8] was correct.'

'You have made it perfectly clear, Mr. Holmes.'

'When I returned to London I called upon the milliner, who at once recognized Straker as an excellent customer, of the name of Darbyshire, who had a very dashing[9] wife with a strong partiality[10] for expensive dresses. I have no doubt that this woman had plunged him over head and ears[11] in debt, and so led him into this miserable plot[12].'

'You have explained all but[13] one thing,' cried the Colonel. 'Where was the horse?'

'Ah, it bolted[14] and was cared for by one of your neighbours. We must have an amnesty in that direction[15], I think. This is Clapham Junction, if I am not mistaken, and we shall be in Victoria in less than ten minutes. If you care[16] to smoke a cigar in our rooms, Colonel, I shall be happy to give you any other details which might interest you.

1. acte malveillant
2. projeté
3. envoyé un coup de sabot
4. fer
5. a entaillé
6. Les chances étaient minces d'élucider ce dernier point
7. Sur quoi se faire la main
8. supposition
9. élégante
10. prédilection
11. jusqu'au cou
12. lamentable machination
13. sauf
14. s'est enfui
15. Sur ce point-là, une amnistie s'impose
16. cela vous dit

The Resident Patient

Sherlock Holmes est sollicité par un confrère du Dr Watson. Un patient a proposé au Dr Percy Trevelyan de financer son cabinet, en échange de quoi il habite lui-même chez le médecin. Or ce patient s'alarme à tout propos, le moindre incident lui inspire une crainte incompréhensible.

In glancing over the somewhat[1] incoherent series of memoirs with which I have endeavoured[2] to illustrate a few of the mental peculiarities of my friend, Mr. Sherlock Holmes, I have been struck by the difficulty which I have experienced[3] in picking out[4] examples which shall in every way answer my purpose[5]. For[6] in those cases in which Holmes has performed some *tour de force*[7] of analytical reasoning, and has demonstrated the value of his peculiar methods of investigation, the facts themselves have often been so slight[8] or so commonplace[9] that I could not feel justified in laying them before the public. On the other hand, it has frequently happened that he has been concerned in some research where the facts have been of the most remarkable and dramatic character, but where the share[10] which he has himself taken in determining their causes has been less pronounced than I, as his biographer, could wish. The small matter[11] which I have chronicled[12] under the heading[13] of *A Study in Scarlet*, and that other later one[14] connected with the loss[15] of the *Gloria Scott*, may serve as examples of this Scylla and Charybdis which are for ever threatening his historian[16]. It may be that, in the business of which I am now about to write, the part which my friend played is not sufficiently accentuated; and yet the whole train of circumstances is so remarkable that I cannot bring myself[17] to omit it entirely from this series.

I cannot be sure of the exact date, for[18] some of my memoranda[19] upon the matter have been mislaid[20], but it must have been towards the end of the first year during which Holmes and I shared chambers[21] in Baker Street. It was boisterous[22] October weather, and we had both remained indoors

1. quelque peu
2. cherché
3. éprouvée
4. à choisir
5. servent mon but à tous points de vue
6. Car,
7. prouesse
8. insignifiants
9. banals
10. la part
11. affaire
12. relatée
13. titre
14. cette autre, plus tard,
15. perte
16. ces périls permanents qu'affronte le chroniqueur, qui n'échappe à l'un que pour tomber dans l'autre
17. me résoudre
18. car
19. notes
20. égarées
21. un appartement
22. agité

1. ébranlée
2. mordant
3. obscures
4. complètement
5. rembruni
6. allant à grands pas jusqu'à
7. virée
8. las
9. en m'emmitouflant
10. nous sommes promenés
11. affluant et refluant
12. s'était défait de
13. vive
14. déduction
15. m'amusait et me captivait
16. coupé
17. La voiture d'un médecin
18. un généraliste
19. à ce que je vois
20. au fait des
21. en osier

all day, I because I feared with my shaken[1] health to face the keen[2] autumn wind, while he was deep in some of those abstruse[3] chemical investigations which absorbed him utterly[4] as long as he was engaged upon them. Towards evening, however, the breaking of a test-tube brought his research to a premature ending, and he sprang up from his chair with an exclamation of impatience and a clouded[5] brow.

'A day's work ruined, Watson,' said he, striding across to[6] the window. 'Ha! the stars are out and the wind has fallen. What do you say to a ramble[7] through London?'

I was weary[8] of our little sitting-room, and gladly acquiesced, muffling myself[9] nose-high against the keen night air. For three hours we strolled about[10] together, watching the ever-changing kaleidoscope of life as it ebbs and flows[11] through Fleet Street and the Strand. Holmes had shaken off[12] his temporary ill-humour, and his characteristic talk, with its keen[13] observance of detail and subtle power of inference[14], held me amused and enthralled[15]. It was ten o'clock before we reached Baker Street again. A brougham[16] was waiting at our door.

'Hum! A doctor's[17] – general practitioner[18], I perceive[19],' said Holmes. 'Not been long in practice, or had much to do. Come to consult us, I fancy! Lucky we came back!'

I was sufficiently conversant with[20] Holmes's methods to be able to follow his reasoning, and to see that the nature and state of the various medical instruments in the wicker[21] basket which hung in the lamp-light inside the brougham had given him the data for his swift deduction. The light in our window above showed that this late visit was indeed intended for us. With some curiosity as to what could have sent a brother medico[1] to us at such an hour, I followed Holmes into our sanctum[2].

A pale, taper-faced[3] man with sandy[4] whiskers[5] rose up from a chair by the fire as we entered. His age may not have been more than three or four and thirty, but his haggard expression and unhealthy hue[6] told[7] of a life which had sapped his strength[8] and robbed him of his youth. His manner was nervous and shy, like that of a sensitive gentleman, and the thin white hand which he laid on the mantelpiece as he rose was that of an artist rather than of a surgeon[9]. His dress[10] was quiet[11] and sombre, a black frock-coat[12], dark trousers, and a touch of colour about his necktie[13].

'Good evening, Doctor,' said Holmes, cheerily[14]; 'I am glad to see that you have only been waiting a very few minutes.'

'You spoke to my coachman, then?'

'No, it was the candle on the side-table that told me. Pray resume your seat[15] and let me know how I can serve you.'

'My name is Doctor Percy Trevelyan,' said our visitor, 'and I live at 403, Brook Street.'

'Are you not the author of a monograph upon obscure nervous lesions?' I asked.

His pale cheeks flushed with pleasure at hearing that his work was known to me.

'I so seldom hear of the work that I thought it was quite dead,' said he. 'My publishers[16] give me a most discouraging account of its sale. You are yourself, I presume, a medical man?'

'A retired Army surgeon.'

'My own hobby has always been nervous disease[17]. I should wish to make it an absolute[18] specialty, but, of course, a man must take what he can get at first. This, however, is beside the question,

1. confrère
2. sanctuaire
3. au visage effilé
4. blond-roux
5. des favoris
6. teint maladif
7. témoignaient
8. sapé ses forces
9. médecin [-chirurgien]
10. vêtements
11. sobres
12. redingote
13. cravate
14. d'un ton enjoué
15. Rasseyez-vous, je vous en prie
16. éditeurs
17. la maladie
18. à part entière

Mr. Sherlock Holmes, and I quite appreciate how valuable your time is. The fact is that a very singular train of events[1] has occurred recently at my house in Brook Street, and tonight they came to such a head[2] that I felt it was quite impossible for me to wait another hour before asking for your advice and assistance.'

Sherlock Holmes sat down and lit his pipe. 'You are very welcome to both,' said he. 'Pray let me have a detailed account of what the circumstances are which have disturbed you.'

'One or two of them are so trivial[3],' said Dr. Trevelyan, 'that really I am almost ashamed to mention them. But the matter is so inexplicable, and the recent turn which it has taken is so elaborate[4], that I shall lay it all before you, and you shall judge what is essential and what is not.

'I am compelled[5], to begin with, to say something of my own college career[6]. I am a London University man, you know, and I am sure you will not think that I am unduly[7] singing my own praises[8] if I say that my student career was considered by my professors to be a very promising one. After I had graduated[9] I continued to devote myself to[10] research, occupying a minor position[11] in King's College Hospital, and I was fortunate enough[12] to excite[13] considerable interest by my research into the pathology of catalepsy, and finally to win the Bruce Pinkerton prize and medal by the monograph on nervous lesions to which your friend has just alluded[14]. I should not go too far[15] if I were to say that there was a general impression at that time that a distinguished[16] career lay before me.

'But the one great stumbling-block[17] lay in my want[18] of capital. As you will readily[19] understand, a specialist who aims[20] high is compelled to start in one of a dozen streets in the Cavendish Square quarter,

1. série d'événements
2. sont arrivés à un point tel
3. insignifiantes
4. complexe
5. forcé
6. cursus universitaire
7. indûment
8. louanges
9. Une fois diplômé,
10. me consacrer
11. petit poste
12. ai eu la chance
13. de susciter
14. vient de faire allusion
15. n'exagérerais pas
16. éminente
17. pierre d'achoppement
18. mon manque
19. aisément
20. vise

all of which entail[1] enormous rents and furnishing expenses. Besides this preliminary outlay[2], he must be prepared to keep himself[3] for some years, and to hire a presentable carriage and horse. To do this was quite beyond my power, and I could only hope that by economy[4] I might in ten years' time save enough to enable me to put up my plate[5]. Suddenly, however, an unexpected incident opened up quite a new prospect[6] to me.

'This was a visit from a gentleman of the name of Blessington, who was a complete stranger to me. He came up into my room one morning, and plunged into business in an instant[7].

' "You are the same Percy Trevelyan who has had so distinguished a career and won a great prize lately?' said he. I bowed[8].

' "Answer me frankly," he continued, "for[9] you will find it to your interest to do so. You have all the cleverness which makes a successful man. Have you the tact?"

'I could not help smiling at[10] the abruptness of the question.

' "I trust that I have my share[11]," I said.

' "Any bad habits[12]? Not drawn towards drink[13], eh?"

' "Really[14], sir!" I cried.

' "Quite right! That's all right! But I was bound to ask[15]. With all these qualities why are you not in practice[16]?"

'I shrugged my shoulders.

' "Come[17], come!" said he, in his bustling way[18]. "It's the old story. More in your brains than in your pocket, eh? What would you say if I were to start you[19] in Brook Street?"

'I stared at him in astonishment.

1. impliquent
2. mise de fonds
3. subvenir à ses besoins
4. en économisant
5. m'établir
6. perspective
7. a abordé d'emblée le but de sa visite
8. me suis incliné en réponse
9. car
10. devant
11. espère en avoir
12. habitudes
13. Pas de penchant pour la boisson
14. Mais enfin
15. me devais de vous poser la question
16. n'avez-vous pas votre propre cabinet
17. Allons
18. à sa façon énergique
19. vous lançais

' "Oh, it's for my sake[1], not for yours," he cried. "I'll be perfectly frank with you, and if it suits you[2] it will suit me very well. I have a few thousands to invest, d'ye[3] see, and I think I'll sink them[4] in you."

' "But why?" I gasped[5].

' "Well, it's just like any other speculation, and safer than most."

' "What am I to do, then?"

' "I'll tell you. I'll take the house, furnish it[6], pay the maids[7], and run the whole place. All you have to do is just to wear out[8] your chair in the consulting-room. I'll let you have pocket-money and everything. Then you hand over to me[9] three-quarters of what you earn[10] and you keep the other quarter for yourself."

'This was the strange proposal, Mr. Holmes, with which the man Blessington approached me. I won't weary you[11] with the account of how we bargained and negotiated[12]. It ended in my moving[13] into the house next Lady Day[14] and starting in practice[15] on very much the same conditions as he had suggested. He came himself to live with me in the character of a[16] resident patient. His heart was weak[17], it appears, and he needed constant medical supervision[18]. He turned the two best rooms on the first floor into a sitting-room and bedroom for himself. He was a man of singular habits, shunning[19] company and very seldom going out. His life was irregular, but in one respect[20] he was regularity itself[21]. Every evening at the same hour he walked into the consulting-room, examined the books[22], put down five[23] and three-pence for every guinea that I had earned, and carried the rest off to the strong box[24] in his own room.

'I may say with confidence[25] that he never had occasion to regret his speculation. From the first[26] it was a success. A few good cases and the reputa-

1. dans mon intérêt
2. cela vous convient,
3. [do you]
4. vais les investir
5. me suis-je écrié, pantelant
6. la meublerai
7. femmes de chambre
8. d'user
9. me remettrez
10. gagnerez
11. vous ennuierai pas
12. récit de nos marchandages et négociations
13. En fin de compte j'ai déménagé
14. le jour de la fête de l'Annonciation
15. ouvert mon cabinet
16. en tant que
17. malade
18. surveillance
19. fuyant
20. sur un point
21. même
22. les comptes
23. [five shillings]
24. coffre-fort
25. assurance
26. Dès le début,

tion which I had won in the hospital brought me rapidly to the front[1], and during the last few years I have made him a rich man.

'So much[2], Mr. Holmes, for my past history and for my relations with Mr. Blessington. It only remains for me now to tell you what has occurred to bring me here tonight.

'Some weeks ago Mr. Blessington came down to me in, as it seemed to me, a state of considerable agitation. He spoke of some burglary[3] which, he said, had been committed in the West End, and he appeared, I remember, to be quite unnecessarily excited about it, declaring that a day should not pass before we should add stronger bolts[4] to our windows and doors. For a week he continued to be in quite a peculiar state of restlessness[5], peering[6] continually out of the windows, and ceasing to take the short walk which had usually been the prelude to his dinner. From his manner[7] it struck me that he was in mortal dread of[8] something or somebody, but when I questioned him upon the point he became so offensive[9] that I was compelled to drop the subject. Gradually as time passed his fears appeared to die away, and he had renewed[10] his former habits, when a fresh event[11] reduced him to the pitiable[12] state of prostration in which he now lies.

'What happened was this. Two days ago I received the letter which I now read to you. Neither address nor date is attached to it.

A Russian nobleman who is now resident in England, it runs[13], *would be glad to avail himself of*[14] *the professional assistance of Dr. Percy Trevelyan. He has been for some years a victim to cataleptic attacks, on which, as is well known, Dr. Trevelyan is an authority. He proposes to call*[15] *at about a quarter*

1. m'ont vite fait connaître
2. Voilà
3. un cambriolage
4. verrous
5. agitation
6. regardant
7. Vu son attitude,
8. redoutait affreusement
9. agressif
10. repris
11. nouvel incident
12. désolant
13. y lit-on
14. bénéficier de
15. se présenter

past six tomorrow evening, if Dr. Trevelyan will make it convenient[1] *to be at home.*

'This letter interested me deeply, because the chief difficulty in the study of catalepsy is the rareness of the disease. You may believe, then, that I was in my consulting-room when, at the appointed hour[2], the page[3] showed in[4] the patient.

'He was an elderly man, thin, demure[5], and commonplace[6] – by no means the conception one forms[7] of a Russian nobleman. I was much more struck by the appearance of his companion. This was a tall young man, surprisingly handsome, with a dark, fierce[8] face, and the limbs and chest[9] of a Hercules. He had his hand under the other's arm as they entered, and helped him to a chair[10] with a tenderness which one would hardly have expected from his appearance.

' "You will excuse my coming in, Doctor," said he to me, speaking English with a slight lisp[11]. 'This is my father, and his health is a matter of the most overwhelming[12] importance to me.'

'I was touched by this filial anxiety. "You would, perhaps, care to[13] remain during the consultation," said I.

' "Not for the world," he cried, with a gesture of horror. "It is more painful to me than I can express. If I were to see my father in one of those dreadful seizures[14], I am convinced that I should never survive it. My own nervous system is an exceptionally sensitive one. With your permission I will remain in the waiting-room while you go into my father's case[15].'

'To this, of course, I assented[16], and the young man withdrew. The patient and I then plunged into a discussion of his case, of which I took exhaustive notes. He was not remarkable for intelligence, and his answers were frequently obscure, which I attributed to his limited acquaintance with

1. peut faire en sorte
2. à l'heure dite
3. groom
4. a fait entrer
5. discret
6. ordinaire
7. loin de l'idée que l'on se fait
8. farouche
9. la carrure
10. l'a aidé à s'asseoir
11. zézaiement
12. extrême
13. souhaitez peut-être
14. crises
15. examinez mon père
16. j'ai consenti

our language[1]. Suddenly, however, as I sat writing he ceased to give any answer at all to my inquiries, and on my turning towards him I was shocked to see that he was sitting bolt upright[2] in his chair, staring at me with a perfectly blank and rigid face[3]. He was again in the grip[4] of his mysterious malady.

'My first feeling, as I have just said, was one of pity and horror. My second, I fear, was rather one of professional satisfaction. I made notes of my patient's pulse[5] and temperature, tested the rigidity of his muscles, and examined his reflexes. There was nothing markedly[6] abnormal in any of these conditions[7], which harmonized[8] with my former experiences. I had obtained good results in such cases by the inhalation of nitrite of amyl[9], and the present[10] seemed an admirable opportunity of testing its virtues. The bottle was downstairs in my laboratory, so, leaving my patient seated in his chair, I ran down to get it. There was some little delay in finding it[11] – five minutes, let us say – and then I returned. Imagine my amazement to find the room empty and the patient gone!

'Of course, my first act was to run into the waiting-room. The son had gone also. The hall door had been closed, but not shut. My page who admits patients is a new boy, and by no means[12] quick. He waits downstairs, and runs up to show patients out[13] when I ring the consulting-room bell. He had heard nothing, and the affair remained a complete mystery. Mr. Blessington came in from his walk shortly afterwards, but I did not say anything to him upon the subject, for[14], to tell the truth, I have got in the way of late[15] of holding as little communication with him as possible.

'Well, I, never thought that I should see anything more of the Russian and his son, so you can imagine my amazement when at the very same hour[16]

1. connaissance limitée de notre langue

2. tout droit

3. air crispé et tout à fait absent

4. sous l'emprise

5. pouls

6. de nettement

7. données

8. concordaient

9. [aujourd'hui classé comme stupéfiant]

10. l'occasion présente

11. J'ai mis quelque temps à trouver le flacon

12. pas du tout

13. pour raccompagner les patients

14. car

15. pris le pli, dernièrement,

16. exactement à la même heure

this evening they both came marching into my consulting-room, just as they had done before.

' "I feel that I owe you a great many apologies for my abrupt departure yesterday, Doctor," said my patient.

' "I confess that I was very much surprised at it," said I.

' "Well, the fact is," he remarked, "that when I recover from these attacks my mind is always very clouded[1] as to[2] all that has gone before[3]. I woke up in a strange room, as it seemed to me, and made my way out into the street in a sort of dazed way[4] when you were absent.

1. embrumé
2. concernant
3. précédé
4. comme hébété

' "And I," said the son, "seeing my father pass the door of the waiting-room, naturally thought that the consultation had come to an end. It was not until we had reached home that I began to realize the true state of affairs."

' "Well," said I, laughing, "there is no harm done[5], except that you puzzled me terribly[6]; so if you, sir, would kindly step into the waiting-room, I shall be happy to continue our consultation, which was brought to so abrupt an ending."

5. il n'y a pas de mal
6. m'avez beaucoup intrigué

'For half an hour or so I discussed the old gentleman's symptoms with him, and then, having prescribed for him[7], I saw him go off on the arm of his son.

7. lui ayant rédigé une ordonnance

'I have told you that Mr. Blessington generally chose this hour of the day for his exercise. He came in shortly afterwards and passed upstairs. An instant later I heard him running down, and he burst[8] into my consulting-room like a man who is mad with panic.

8. a fait irruption

' "Who has been in my room?" he cried.

' "No one," said I.

' "It's a lie!" he yelled[9]. "Come up and look."

9. a-t-il hurlé

'I passed over[1] the grossness[2] of his language, as he seemed half out of his mind with fear[3]. When I went upstairs with him he pointed to several footprints upon the light carpet.

' "D'you mean to say those are mine?" he cried.

'They were certainly very much larger than any which he could have made, and were evidently quite fresh[4]. It rained hard this afternoon, as you know, and my patients were the only people who called[5]. It must have been the case, then, that the man in the waiting-room had for some unknown reason, while I was busy with the other, ascended to the room of my resident patient. Nothing had been touched or taken, but there were the footprints to prove that the intrusion was an undoubted[6] fact.

'Mr. Blessington seemed more excited over the matter than I should have thought possible, though, of course, it was enough to disturb anybody's peace of mind. He actually sat crying[7] in an armchair, and I could hardly get him to speak coherently. It was his suggestion that I should come round to you[8], and of course I at once saw the propriety[9] of it, for certainly the incident is a very singular one, though he appears to completely overrate[10] its importance. If you would only come back with me in my brougham, you would at least be able to soothe him[11], though I can hardly hope that you will be able to explain this remarkable occurrence[12].'

Sherlock Holmes had listened to this long narrative with an intentness[13] which showed me that his interest was keenly aroused. His face was as impassive as ever, but his lids had drooped[14] more heavily over his eyes, and his smoke had curled up more thickly from his pipe to emphasize[15] each curious episode in the doctor's tale. As our visitor concluded Holmes sprang up without a word, handed me my

1. n'ai pas relevé
2. grossièreté
3. à moitié mort de frayeur
4. manifestement toutes récentes
5. à me rendre visite
6. indubitable
7. s'est même mis à pleurer
8. vienne vous voir
9. bien-fondé
10. surestimer
11. l'apaiser
12. incident
13. air absorbé
14. paupières s'étaient abaissées
15. pour souligner

hat, picked up his own from the table, and followed Dr. Trevelyan to the door. Within a quarter of an hour we had been dropped at the door of the physician's[1] residence in Brook Street, one of those sombre, flat-faced[2] houses which one associates with a West End practice[3]. A small page admitted us, and we began at once to ascend the broad, well-carpeted stair.

But a singular interruption brought us to a standstill[4]. The light at the top was suddenly whisked out[5], and from the darkness came a reedy[6], quavering[7] voice.

'I have a pistol,' it cried; 'I give you my word that I'll fire if you come any nearer.'

'This really grows outrageous[8], Mr. Blessington,' cried Dr. Trevelyan.

'Oh, then it is you, Doctor?' said the voice, with a great heave[9] of relief[10]. 'But those other gentlemen, are they what they pretend to be?'

We were conscious of a long scrutiny out of the darkness.

'Yes, yes, it's all right,' said the voice at last. 'You can come up, and I am sorry if my precautions have annoyed you.'

He re-lit the stair gas[11] as he spoke, and we saw before us a singular-looking man, whose appearance, as well as his voice, testified to[12] his jangled nerves[13]. He was very fat, but had apparently at some time been much fatter, so that the skin hung about his face in loose pouches[14], like the cheeks of a bloodhound[15]. He was of a sickly[16] colour, and his thin sandy hair seemed to bristle up[17] with the intensity of his emotion. In his hand he held a pistol, but he thrust it into his pocket as we advanced.

'Good evening, Mr. Holmes,' said he; 'I am sure I am very much obliged to you for coming round. No one ever needed your advice more than I do. I sup-

1. du médecin
2. à façade sans saillie
3. aux cabinets médicaux du West End
4. nous immobilisa
5. s'éteignit brusquement
6. fluette
7. tremblotante
8. scandaleux
9. soupir
10. soulagement
11. lampe à gaz
12. témoignaient de
13. ses nerfs à vif
14. en bajoues flasques
15. dogue
16. maladive
17. se hérisser

pose that Dr. Trevelyan has told you of this most unwarrantable[1] intrusion into my rooms.'

'Quite so,' said Holmes. 'Who are these two men, Mr. Blessington, and why do they wish to molest you[2]?'

'Well, well,' said the resident patient, in a nervous fashion, 'of course, it is hard to say that. You can hardly expect me to answer that, Mr. Holmes.'

'Do you mean that you don't know?'

'Come in here, if you please. Just have the kindness to step in here.'

He led the way[3] into his bedroom, which was large and comfortably furnished.

'You see that,' said he, pointing to a big black box[4] at the end of his bed. 'I have never been a very rich man, Mr. Holmes – never made but one[5] investment in my life, as Dr. Trevelyan would tell you. But I don't believe in bankers. I would never trust a banker, Mr. Holmes. Between ourselves, what little I have is in that box, so you can understand what it means to me when unknown people force themselves into my rooms[6].'

Holmes looked at Blessington in his questioning way[7], and shook his head.

'I cannot possibly advise you if you try to deceive me[8],' said he.

'But I have told you everything.'

Holmes turned on his heel with a gesture of disgust. 'Good night, Dr. Trevelyan,' said he.

'And no advice for me?' cried Blessington, in a breaking[9] voice.

'My advice to you, sir, is to speak the truth.'

A minute later we were in the street and walking for home. We had crossed Oxford Street, and were half-way down Harley Street before I could get a word from my companion.

1. injustifiable
2. vous importuner
3. nous conduisit
4. coffre noir
5. n'ai fait qu'un
6. s'introduisent de force chez moi
7. de son air interrogateur
8. de me tromper
9. brisée

'Sorry to bring you out on such a fool's errand[1], Watson,' he said at last. 'It is an interesting case, too[2], at the bottom of it[3].'

'I can make little of it[4],' I confessed.

'Well, it is quite evident that there are two men – more, perhaps, but at least two – who are determined for some reason to get at[5] this fellow Blessington. I have no doubt in my mind that both on the first and on the second occasion that young man penetrated to Blessington's room, while his confederate[6], by an ingenious device[7], kept the doctor from interfering[8].'

'And the catalepsy!'

'A fraudulent[9] imitation, Watson, though I should hardly dare[10] to hint as much[11] to our specialist. It is a very easy complaint[12] to imitate. I have done it myself.'

'And then?'

'By the purest chance[13] Blessington was out on each occasion. Their reason for choosing so unusual an hour for a consultation was obviously to insure that there should be[14] no other patient in the waiting-room. It just happened[15], however, that this hour coincided with Blessington's constitutional[16], which seems to show that they were not very well acquainted with[17] his daily routine. Of course, if they had been merely[18] after plunder[19] they would at least have made some attempt to search for it. Besides, I can read in a man's eye when it is his own skin that he is frightened for. It is inconceivable that this fellow could have made two such vindictive enemies as these appear to be without knowing of it. I hold it, therefore, to be certain[20] that he does know who these men are, and that for reasons of his own he suppresses it[21]. It is just possible that tomorrow may find him in a more communicative mood.'

1. de vous avoir fait venir en pure perte
2. d'ailleurs
3. en réalité
4. n'y comprends pas grand-chose
5. s'en prendre à
6. complice
7. stratagème
8. empêchait le docteur d'intervenir
9. trompeuse
10. ne m'aventurerais pas à
11. le laisser entendre
12. mal
13. le plus grand des hasards
14. s'assurer qu'il n'y ait
15. Il s'est trouvé
16. la promenade quotidienne
17. très au courant de
18. simplement
19. à la recherche d'un butin
20. C'est pourquoi je suis convaincu
21. le tait

'Is there not one alternative,' I suggested, 'grotesquely improbable, no doubt, but still just conceivable? Might the whole story of the cataleptic Russian and his son be a concoction[1] of Dr. Trevelyan's, who has, for his own purposes, been in Blessington's rooms?'

I saw in the gaslight that Holmes wore an amused smile at this brilliant departure[2] of mine.

'My dear fellow,' said he, 'it was one of the first solutions which occurred to me, but I was soon able to corroborate the doctor's tale. This young man has left prints upon the stair carpet which made it quite superfluous for me to ask to see those which he had made in the room. When I tell you that his shoes were square-toed[3], instead of being pointed like Blessington's, and were quite an inch and a third longer than the doctor's, you will acknowledge[4] that there can be no doubt as to his individuality[5]. But we may sleep on it now[6], for I shall be surprised if we do not hear something further[7] from Brook Street in the morning.'

Sherlock Holmes's prophecy was soon fulfilled[8], and in a dramatic fashion. At half-past seven next morning, in the first dim glimmer of daylight[9], I found him standing by my bedside in his dressing-gown.

'There's a brougham waiting for us, Watson,' said he.

'What's the matter, then?'

'The Brook Street business.'

'Any fresh news?'

'Tragic but ambiguous,' said he, pulling up the blind[10]. 'Look at this – a sheet from a notebook with "For God's sake[11], come at once – P. T." scrawled[12] upon it in pencil. Our friend the doctor was

1. fable

2. innovation

3. à bouts carrés

4. reconnaîtrez

5. qu'il s'agit de quelqu'un d'autre

6. nous en tiendrons là ce soir

7. n'avons pas de nouvelles

8. réalisée

9. toute première lueur du jour

10. store

11. Pour l'amour du ciel

12. griffonné

1. en grande difficulté
2. quelle histoire
3. à ses tempes
4. siffla
5. s'est pendu
6. le malheureux
7. crochet
8. était suspendue
9. du coffre que justement
10. avachissement
11. donnait
12. pendait
13. à peine
14. plumé
15. d'autant plus

hard put to it[1] when he wrote this. Come along, my dear fellow, for it's an urgent call.'

In a quarter of an hour or so we were back at the physician's house. He came running out to meet us with a face of horror.

'Oh, such a business[2]!' he cried, with his hands to his temples[3].

'What, then?'

'Blessington has committed suicide!'

Holmes whistled[4].

'Yes, he hanged himself[5] during the night.'

We had entered, and the doctor had preceded us into what was evidently his waiting-room.

'I really hardly know what I am doing,' he cried. 'The police are already upstairs. It has shaken me most dreadfully.'

'When did you find it out?'

'He has a cup of tea taken in to him early every morning. When the maid entered about seven, there the unfortunate fellow[6] was hanging in the middle of the room. He had tied his cord to the hook[7] on which the heavy lamp used to hang[8], and he had jumped off from the top of the very box that[9] he showed us yesterday.'

Holmes stood for a moment in deep thought.

'With your permission,' said he at last, 'I should like to go upstairs and look into the matter.' We both ascended, followed by the doctor.

It was a dreadful sight which met us as we entered the bedroom door. I have spoken of the impression of flabbiness[10] which this man Blessington conveyed[11]. As he dangled[12] from the hook it was exaggerated and intensified until he was scarce[13] human in his appearance. The neck was drawn out like a plucked[14] chicken's, making the rest of him seem the more[15] obese and unnatural by the contrast.

He was clad only in his long nightdress, and his swollen ankles and ungainly[1] feet protruded[2] starkly[3] from beneath it. Beside him stood a smart-looking police inspector, who was taking notes in a pocket-book.

'Ah, Mr. Holmes,' said he, heartily[4], as my friend entered. 'I am delighted to see you.'

'Good morning, Lanner,' answered Holmes. 'You won't think me an intruder, I am sure. Have you heard of the events which led up to this affair?'

'Yes, I heard something of them.'

'Have you formed any opinion?'

'As far as I can see, the man has been driven out of his senses by fright[5]. The bed has been well slept in[6], you see. There's his impression deep enough[7]. It's about five in the morning, you know, that suicides are most common. That would be about his time for hanging himself. It seems to have been a very deliberate[8] affair.'

'I should say that he has been dead about three hours, judging by the rigidity of the muscles,' said I.

'Noticed anything peculiar about the room?' asked Holmes.

'Found a screwdriver[9] and some screws on the wash-hand stand[10]. Seems to have smoked heavily[11] during the night, too. Here are four cigar ends that I picked out of the fireplace.'

'Hum!' said Holmes. 'Have you got his cigar-holder[12]?'

'No, I have seen none.'

'His cigar-case[13], then?'

'Yes, it was in his coat pocket.'

Holmes opened it and smelled the single cigar which it contained.

'Oh, this is a Havana, and these others are cigars of the peculiar sort which are imported by the Dutch[14] from their East Indian[15] colonies. They

1. disgracieux
2. dépassaient
3. de façon frappante
4. chaleureusement
5. la peur lui a fait perdre la tête
6. Il a passé une bonne partie de la nuit dans ce lit
7. On voit bien la marque de son corps
8. mûrement réfléchie
9. tournevis
10. meuble de toilette
11. beaucoup
12. fume-cigare
13. étui à cigares
14. Hollandais
15. des Indes orientales

1. marque
2. loupe de poche
3. de très bonnes dents
4. soigneusement prémédité
5. commis de sang-froid
6. d'une façon aussi maladroite que la pendaison
7. supplémentaire
8. tablette de la cheminée
9. se déclare
10. triste dépouille
11. respectueusement
12. a été prélevée là-dessus
13. tout un rouleau
14. avait une peur maladive

are usually wrapped in straw, you know, and are thinner for their length than any other brand[1].' He picked up the four ends and examined them with his pocket lens[2].

'Two of these have been smoked from a holder and two without,' said he. 'Two have been cut by a not very sharp knife, and two have had the ends bitten off by a set of excellent teeth[3]. This is no suicide, Mr. Lanner. It is a very deeply-planned[4] and cold-blooded[5] murder.'

'Impossible!' cried the inspector.

'And why?'

'Why should anyone murder a man in so clumsy a fashion as by hanging him[6]?'

'That is what we have to find out.'

'How could they get in?'

'Through the front door.'

'It was barred in the morning.'

'Then it was barred after them.'

'How do you know?'

'I saw their traces. Excuse me a moment, and I may be able to give you some further[7] information about it.'

He went over to the door, and turning the lock he examined it in his methodical fashion. Then he took out the key, which was on the inside, and inspected that also. The bed, the carpet, the chairs, the mantelpiece[8], the dead body, and the rope were each in turn examined, until at last he professed himself[9] satisfied, and with my aid and that of the inspector cut down the wretched object[10], and laid it reverently[11] under a sheet.

'How about this rope?' he asked.

'It is cut off this[12],' said Dr. Trevelyan, drawing a large coil[13] from under the bed. 'He was morbidly nervous[14] of fire, and always kept this beside him, so that he might escape by the window in case the stairs were burning.'

'That must have saved them trouble[1],' said Holmes, thoughtfully[2]. 'Yes, the actual[3] facts are very plain[4], and I shall be surprised if by the afternoon I cannot give you the reasons for them as well. I will take this photograph of Blessington which I see upon the mantelpiece, as it may help me in my inquiries.'

'But you have told us nothing,' cried the doctor.

'Oh, there can be no doubt as to the sequence[5] of events,' said Holmes. 'There were three of them in it: the young man, the old man, and a third to whose identity I have no clue[6]. The first two, I need hardly remark[7], are the same who masqueraded as[8] the Russian Count and his son, so we can give a very full description of them. They were admitted by a confederate inside the house. If I might offer you a word of advice[9], Inspector, it would be to arrest the page, who, as I understand, has only recently come into your service, Doctor.'

'The young imp[10] cannot be found,' said Dr. Trevelyan; 'the maid and the cook have just been searching for him.'

Holmes shrugged his shoulders.

'He has played a not unimportant[11] part[12] in this drama,' said he. 'The three men having ascended the stair, which they did on tiptoe[13], the elder man first, the younger man second, and the unknown man in the rear[14] –'

'My dear Holmes!' I ejaculated[15].

'Oh, there could be no question[16] as to the superimposing[17] of the footmarks. I had the advantage of learning which was which[18] last night. They ascended then to Mr. Blessington's room, the door of which they found to be locked. With the help of a wire[19], however, they forced round the key. Even

1. leur faciliter le travail
2. pensivement
3. proprement dits
4. clairs
5. enchaînement
6. dont rien ne me laisse deviner l'identité
7. ai-je besoin de le préciser
8. se sont fait passer pour
9. conseil
10. coquin
11. pas du tout anodin
12. rôle
13. sur la pointe des pieds
14. à l'arrière
15. me récriai-je
16. doute
17. quant au chevauchement
18. apprendre à les identifier
19. fil de fer

without a lens, you will perceive by the scratches on this ward[1] where the pressure was applied.

'On entering the room, their first proceeding must have been[2] to gag[3] Mr. Blessington. He may have been asleep, or he may have been so paralysed with terror as to have been unable to cry out. These walls are thick, and it is conceivable that his shriek[4], if he had time to utter one[5], was unheard.

'Having secured[6] him, it is evident to me that a consultation[7] of some sort was held. Probably it was something in the nature of a judicial proceeding[8]. It must have lasted[9] for some time, for it was then that these cigars were smoked. The older man sat in that wicker[10] chair: it was he who used the cigar-holder. The younger man sat over yonder[11]: he knocked his ash off against the chest of drawers[12]. The third fellow paced up and down[13]. Blessington, I think, sat upright in the bed, but of that I cannot be absolutely certain.

'Well, it ended by their taking Blessington and hanging him. The matter was so prearranged that it is my belief that they brought with them some sort of block[14] or pulley[15] which might serve as a gallows[16]. That screwdriver and those screws were, as I conceive[17], for fixing it up. Seeing the hook, however, they naturally saved themselves[18] the trouble[19]. Having finished their work they made off[20], and the door was barred behind them by their confederate.'

We had all listened with the deepest interest to this sketch of the night's doings[21], which Holmes had deduced from signs so subtle and minute[22], that even when he had pointed them out to us, we could scarcely[23] follow him in his reasonings. The inspector hurried away on the instant to make inquiries about the page, while Holmes and I returned to Baker Street for breakfast.

1. encoche
2. ils ont sans doute commencé par
3. bâillonner
4. cri
5. de crier
6. ligoté
7. conciliabule
8. procès
9. durer
10. en osier
11. là-bas
12. commode
13. allait et venait
14. palan
15. poulie
16. de potence
17. à mon avis
18. se sont épargné
19. cette peine
20. sont partis
21. bref récit de ce qui s'était passé durant la nuit
22. infimes
23. à peine

'I'll be back by three,' said he when we had finished our meal. 'Both the inspector and the doctor will meet me here at that hour, and I hope by that time to have cleared up any little obscurity[1] which the case may still present.'

Our visitors arrived at the appointed time[2], but it was a quarter to four before my friend put in an appearance[3]. From his expression as he entered, however, I could see that all had gone well with him[4].

'Any news, Inspector?'

'We have got the boy, sir.'

'Excellent, and I have got the men.'

'You have got them!' we cried all three.

'Well, at least I have got their identity. This so-called Blessington is, as I expected, well known at headquarters[5], and so are his assailants[6]. Their names are Biddle, Hayward, and Moffat.'

'The Worthingdon bank gang,' cried the inspector.

'Precisely,' said Holmes.

'Then Blessington must have been Sutton?'

'Exactly,' said Holmes.

'Why, that makes it as clear as crystal,' said the inspector.

But Trevelyan and I looked at each other in bewilderment[7].

'You must surely remember the great Worthingdon bank business,' said Holmes; 'five men were in it, these four and a fifth called Cartwright. Tobin, the caretaker[8], was murdered, and the thieves got away with seven thousand pounds. This was in 1875. They were all five arrested, but the evidence against them was by no means conclusive[9]. This Blessington, or Sutton, who was the worst of the gang, turned informer[10]. On his evidence[11], Cartwright was hanged and the other three got fifteen years apiece[12]. When they got out the other day, which was some years

1. point obscur
2. à l'heure dite
3. que mon ami fasse son apparition
4. de son côté
5. à la police centrale
6. agresseurs
7. avec stupeur
8. gardien
9. concluante
10. est devenu indic
11. Sur la foi de sa déposition
12. chacun

before their full term[1], they set themselves[2], as you perceive, to hunt down[3] the traitor and to avenge the death of their comrade upon him. Twice they tried to get at him[4] and failed; a third time, you see, it came off[5]. Is there anything further[6] which I can explain, Dr. Trevelyan?'

'I think you have made it all remarkably clear,' said the doctor. 'No doubt the day on which he was so perturbed was the day when he had read of their release[7] in the newspapers.'

'Quite so. His talk about a burglary was the merest blind[8].'

'But why could he not tell you this?'

'Well, my dear sir, knowing the vindictive[9] character of his old associates, he was trying to hide his own identity from everybody as long as he could. His secret was a shameful one, and he could not bring himself to[10] divulge it. However, wretch as he was[11], he was still living under the shield[12] of British law, and I have no doubt, Inspector, that you will see that, though that shield may fail to guard, the sword[13] of justice is still there to avenge.'

Such were the singular circumstances in connection with the resident patient and the Brook Street doctor. From that night nothing has been seen of the three murderers by the police, and it is surmised[14] at Scotland Yard that they were among the passengers of the ill-fated[15] steamer *Norah Creina*, which was lost some years ago with all hands[16] upon the Portuguese coast, some leagues to the north of Oporto. The proceedings[17] against the page broke down[18] for want of evidence[19], and the *Brook Street Mystery,* as it was called, has never, until now, been fully dealt with[20] in any public print[21].

1. le plein accomplissement de leur peine
2. se sont mis
3. à traquer
4. s'en prendre à lui
5. ils ont réussi
6. quoi que ce soit d'autre
7. sortie de prison
8. un simple leurre
9. rancunier
10. se résoudre à
11. aussi criminel qu'il fût
12. rempart
13. glaive
14. on présume
15. au destin tragique
16. tout son équipage
17. L'instruction
18. fut abandonnée
19. faute de preuves
20. relatée dans le détail
21. publication

The Naval Treaty

Sherlock Holmes et le docteur Watson nous emmènent dans le monde feutré des diplomates.

Si le seul exemplaire d'un traité secret vient à s'évaporer, les risques pour le Royaume-Uni ne sont pas minces ; c'est de guerre et de paix qu'il s'agit.

THE JULY WHICH immediately succeeded my marriage was made memorable by three cases[1] of interest in which I had the privilege of being associated with Sherlock Holmes, and of studying his methods. I find them recorded in my notes under the headings[2] of *The Adventure of the Second Stain*[3], *The Adventure of the Naval Treaty*, and *The Adventure of the Tired Captain*. The first of these, however, deals with[4] interests of such importance, and implicates so many of the first families in the kingdom, that for many years it will be impossible to make it public. No case, however, in which Holmes was ever engaged has illustrated the value of his analytical methods so clearly or has impressed those who were associated with him so deeply. I still retain[5] an almost verbatim[6] report of the interview in which he demonstrated the true facts of the case to Monsieur Dubuque, of the Paris Police, and Fritz von Waldbaum, the well-known specialist of Dantzig, both of whom had wasted[7] their energies upon what proved to be side-issues[8]. The new century will have come, however, before the story can be safely told. Meanwhile[9], I pass on to the second upon my list, which promised also, at one time, to be of national importance, and was marked by several incidents which give it a quite unique character.

During my school-days I had been intimately associated with[10] a lad named Percy Phelps, who was of much[11] the same age as myself, though he was two classes ahead of me. He was a very brilliant boy, and carried away every prize which the school had to offer, finishing his exploits by winning a scholarship[12], which sent him on to continue his triumphant career at Cambridge. He was[13], I remember,

1. affaires
2. titres
3. tache
4. touche à
5. conserve
6. [*mot pour mot* ; latin]
7. gaspillé
8. des questions secondaires
9. En attendant
10. lié à
11. avait pour ainsi dire
12. bourse
13. avait

1. des relations haut placées
2. tapageuse
3. ne lui valut rien de bon
4. grisant
5. le harceler
6. tibias
7. bâton de guichet [au cricket]
8. fit ses débuts
9. aptitudes
10. entregent
11. dont il disposait
12. me rappela

extremely well connected[1] and even when we were all little boys together, we knew that his mother's brother was Lord Holdhurst, the great Conservative politician. This gaudy[2] relationship did him little good[3] at school; on the contrary, it seemed rather a piquant thing[4] to us to chevy him[5] about the playground and hit him over the shins[6] with a wicket[7]. But it was another thing when he came out[8] into the world. I heard vaguely that his abilities[9] and the influence[10] which he commanded[11] had won him a good position at the Foreign Office, and then he passed completely out of my mind until the following letter recalled[12] his existence:

'BRIARBRAE, WOKING.

13. le Têtard
14. en seconde
15. en quatrième
16. poste
17. confiance
18. distinction
19. anéantir
20. Au cas où
21. tu accéderais à ma demande
22. suis tout juste remis
23. auprès de moi

'My dear Watson, –

I have no doubt that you can remember Tadpole[13] Phelps, who was in the fifth form[14] when you were in the third[15]. It is possible even that you may have heard that, through my uncle's influence, I obtained a good appointment[16] at the Foreign Office, and that I was in a situation of trust[17] and honour[18] until a horrible misfortune came suddenly to blast[19] my career.

There is no use writing the details of that dreadful event. In the event of[20] your acceding to my request[21], it is probable that I shall have to narrate them to you. I have only just recovered[22] from nine weeks of brain fever, and am still exceedingly weak. Do you think that you could bring your friend, Mr. Holmes, down to see me[23]? I should like to have his opinion of the case, though the authorities assure me that nothing more can be done. Do try to bring him down, and as soon as possible. Every minute seems an hour while I live in this horrible suspense. Assure him that, if I have not asked his advice sooner, it was not because I did not appreciate his talents, but because I have been off my head[1] *ever since the blow fell. Now I am clear again, though I dare not think of it too much for fear of a relapse*[2]. *I am still so weak that I have to write, as you see, by dictating. Do try and bring him.*

'Your old schoolfellow,'
PERCY PHELPS.'

There was something that touched me as I read this letter, something pitiable[3] in the reiterated appeals to bring Holmes. So moved[4] was I that, even if it had been a difficult matter, I should have tried it; but, of course, I knew well that Holmes loved his art so[5], that he was ever as ready to bring his aid as his client could be to receive it. My wife agreed with me that not a moment should be lost in laying the matter before him[6], and so, within an hour of[7] breakfast-time, I found myself back once more in the old rooms in Baker Street.

Holmes was seated at his side-table[8] clad in[9] his dressing-gown and working hard over a chemical investigation[10]. A large curved retort[11] was boiling furiously in the bluish flame of a Bunsen burner[12], and the distilled drops[13] were condensing into a two-litre measure[14]. My friend hardly glanced up as I entered, and I, seeing that his investigation must be of importance, seated myself in an armchair and waited. He dipped[15] into this bottle or that, drawing out a few drops of each with his glass pipette, and finally brought a test-tube[16] containing a solution over to the table. In his right hand he had a slip of litmus-paper[17].

1. n'avais plus toute ma tête
2. rechute
3. poignant
4. touché
5. à tel point
6. pour lui soumettre l'affaire
7. moins d'une heure après
8. petite table
9. vêtu de
10. expérience de chimie
11. cornue
12. bec Bunsen
13. gouttes
14. verre doseur
15. plongeait
16. éprouvette
17. bande de papier au tournesol [colorants indicateurs du pH d'une solution]

1. au moment crucial
2. vira
3. terne
4. C'est bien ce que je pensais
5. babouche persane
6. griffonna rapidement
7. garçon de courses
8. retiennent
9. banal
10. j'imagine
11. messager [le pétrel-tempête était réputé ne venir à terre qu'en cas de violente tempête]
12. m'écriai-je
13. très proche de
14. que ce soit en bien ou en mal,
15. une situation aussi désastreuse
16. eûmes la chance
17. bois de sapins

'You come at a crisis[1], Watson,' said he. 'If this paper remains blue, all is well. If it turns red, it means a man's life.' He dipped it into the test-tube, and it flushed[2] at once into a dull[3], dirty crimson. 'Hum! I thought as much[4]!' he cried. 'I shall be at your service in one instant, Watson. You will find tobacco in the Persian slipper[5].' He turned to his desk and scribbled off[6] several telegrams, which were handed over to the page-boy[7]. Then he threw himself down in the chair opposite, and drew up his knees until his fingers clasped round[8] his long, thin shins.

'A very commonplace[9] little murder,' said he. 'You've got something better, I fancy[10]. You are the stormy petrel[11] of crime, Watson. What is it?'

I handed him the letter, which he read with the most concentrated attention.

'It does not tell us very much, does it?' he remarked, as he handed it back to me.

'Hardly anything.'

'And yet the writing is of interest.'

'But the writing is not his own.'

'Precisely. It is a woman's.'

'A man's surely!' I cried[12].

'No, a woman's; and a woman of rare character. You see, at the commencement of an investigation, it is something to know that your client is in close contact with[13] someone who for good or evil[14] has an exceptional nature. My interest is already awakened in the case. If you are ready, we will start at once for Woking and see this diplomatist who is in such evil case[15], and the lady to whom he dictates his letters.'

We were fortunate enough[16] to catch an early train at Waterloo, and in a little under an hour we found ourselves among the fir-woods[17] and the heather[1] of Woking. Briarbrae proved to[2] be a large detached[3] house standing in extensive grounds[4], within a few minutes' walk of the station. On sending in[5] our cards we were shown[6] into an elegantly appointed[7] drawing-room, where we were joined in a few minutes by a rather stout[8] man, who received us with much hospitality. His age may have been nearer forty than thirty, but his cheeks were so ruddy[9] and his eyes so merry[10], that he still conveyed[11] the impression of a plump[12] and mischievous[13] boy.

'I am so glad that you have come,' said he, shaking our hands with effusion. 'Percy has been inquiring for you all the morning. Ah, poor old chap, he clings to any straw[14]. His father and mother asked me to see you, for[15] the mere mention[16] of the subject is very painful to them.'

'We have had no details yet,' observed Holmes. 'I perceive that you are not yourself a member of the family.'

Our acquaintance[17] looked surprised, and then glancing down he began to laugh.

'Of course you saw the "J. H." monogram on my locket[18],' said he. 'For a moment I thought you had done something clever. Joseph Harrison is my name, and as Percy is to marry my sister Annie, I shall at least be a relation[19] by marriage. You will find my sister in his room, for she has nursed him hand-and-foot[20] these two months back[21]. Perhaps we had better go in at once, for I know how impatient he is.'

The chamber into which we were shown was on the same floor as the drawing-room. It was furnished partly as a sitting- and partly as a bedroom, with flowers arranged daintily[22] in every nook and corner[23]. A young man, very pale and worn[24], was lying upon a sofa near the open window, through

1. bruyère
2. s'avéra
3. isolée
4. une vaste propriété
5. Sur présentation de
6. introduits
7. meublé
8. corpulent
9. vermeilles
10. rieurs
11. donnait toujours
12. rondouillard
13. malicieux
14. se raccroche au moindre espoir
15. car
16. simple évocation
17. nouvelle connaissance
18. médaillon
19. parent
20. a été aux petits soins avec lui
21. ces deux derniers mois
22. avec délicatesse
23. le moindre recoin
24. las

which came the rich scent[1] of the garden and the balmy[2] summer air. A woman was sitting beside him, and rose as we entered.

'Shall I leave, Percy?' she asked.

He clutched[3] her hand to detain her[4]. 'How are you, Watson?' said he, cordially. 'I should never have known you[5] under that moustache, and I daresay[6] you would not be prepared[7] to swear to me[8]. This, I presume, is your celebrated[9] friend, Mr. Sherlock Holmes?'

I introduced him[10] in a few words, and we both sat down. The stout young man had left us, but his sister still remained, with her hand in that of the invalid[11]. She was a striking-looking woman, a little short and thick for symmetry[12], but with a beautiful olive complexion[13], large, dark Italian eyes, and a wealth of deep black hair[14]. Her rich tints made the white face of her companion the more[15] worn and haggard by the contrast[16].

'I won't waste your time,' said he, raising himself upon the sofa. 'I'll plunge into the matter without further preamble[17]. I was a happy and successful man, Mr. Holmes, and on the eve of being married[18], when a sudden and dreadful misfortune wrecked[19] all my prospects in life[20].

'I was, as Watson may have told you, in the Foreign Office, and through the influence of my uncle, Lord Holdhurst, I rose rapidly to a responsible position[21]. When my uncle became Foreign Minister in this Administration he gave me several missions of trust, and as I always brought them to a successful conclusion[22], he came at last to have the utmost[23] confidence[24] in my ability[25] and tact.

'Nearly ten weeks ago – to be more accurate[26], on the 23rd of May – he called me into his private room and, after complimenting me upon the good

1. fragrances
2. parfumé
3. agrippa
4. la retenir
5. ne t'aurais jamais reconnu
6. suppose
7. que tu ne serais pas prêt
8. à jurer que c'est bien moi
9. illustre
10. le présentai
11. malade
12. des proportions harmonieuses
13. teint mat
14. abondante chevelure d'un noir profond
15. d'autant plus
16. par comparaison
17. autre préambule
18. sur le point de me marier
19. est venu ruiner
20. perspectives d'avenir
21. poste de responsabilité
22. m'en suis toujours acquitté avec succès
23. la plus grande
24. confiance
25. compétences
26. précis

work which I had done, informed me that he had a new commission of trust[1] for me to execute.

' "This," said he, taking a grey roll of paper from his bureau, "is the original of that secret treaty between England and Italy, of which, I regret to say, some rumours have already got[2] into the public Press. It is of enormous importance that nothing further should leak out[3]. The French or Russian Embassies would pay an immense sum to learn the contents[4] of these papers. They should not leave my bureau were it not that it is[5] absolutely necessary to have them copied. You have a desk in your office?"

' "Yes, sir."

' "Then take the treaty and lock it up there. I shall give directions that[6] you may remain behind when the others go, so that you may copy it at your leisure[7], without fear of being overlooked[8]. When you have finished, re-lock both the original and the draft[9] in the desk, and hand them over to me personally tomorrow morning."

'I took the papers and–'

'Excuse me an instant,' said Holmes; 'were you alone during this conversation?'

'Absolutely.'

'In a large room?'

'Thirty feet each way.'

'In the centre?'

'Yes, about it[10].'

'And speaking low?'

'My uncle's voice is always remarkably low. I hardly spoke at all.'

'Thank you,' said Holmes, shutting his eyes; 'pray[11] go on.'

'I did exactly what he had indicated, and waited until the other clerks[12] had departed. One of them in

1. mission de confiance
2. filtré
3. qu'il n'y ait pas d'autre fuite
4. le contenu
5. s'il n'était
6. des instructions pour que
7. tout à loisir
8. à l'abri des regards
9. votre copie
10. à peu près
11. veuillez
12. employés

my room, Charles Gorot, had some arrears of work[1] to make up[2], so I left him there and went out to dine. When I returned he was gone. I was anxious to hurry[3] my work, for I knew that Joseph, the Mr. Harrison whom you saw just now, was in town, and that he would travel down to Woking by the eleven o'clock train, and I wanted if possible to catch it.

'When I came to examine the treaty I saw at once that it was of such importance that my uncle had been guilty of no exaggeration[4] in what he had said. Without going into details, I may say that it defined the position of Great Britain towards the Triple Alliance, and foreshadowed[5] the policy which this country would pursue in the event of[6] the French fleet[7] gaining a complete ascendency over that[8] of Italy in the Mediterranean. The questions treated in it were purely naval. At the end were the signatures of the high dignitaries who had signed it. I glanced my eyes over it[9], and then settled down to[10] my task of copying.

'It was a long document, written in the French language, and containing twenty-six separate articles[11]. I copied as quickly as I could, but at nine o'clock I had only done nine articles, and it seemed hopeless for me to attempt to catch my train. I was feeling drowsy[12] and stupid[13], partly from my dinner and also from the effects of a long day's work. A cup of coffee would clear my brain[14]. A commissionaire[15] remains all night in a little lodge[16] at the foot of the stairs, and is in the habit[17] of making coffee at his spirit-lamp[18] for any of the officials[19] who may be working overtime[20]. I rang the bell, therefore[21], to summon him[22].

'To my surprise, it was a woman who answered the summons[23], a large, coarse-faced[24], elderly woman, in an apron[25]. She explained that she was

1. du travail en retard
2. à rattraper
3. avais hâte d'en finir avec
4. n'avait aucunement exagéré
5. annonçait
6. au cas où
7. flotte
8. surclasserait totalement celle
9. l'ai parcouru du regard
10. me suis attelé à
11. clauses
12. somnolent
13. abruti
14. m'éclaircirait les idées
15. portier
16. loge
17. a pour coutume
18. lampe à alcool
19. fonctionnaires
20. feraient des heures supplémentaires
21. par conséquent
22. le faire venir
23. à l'appel
24. au visage grossier
25. en tablier

the commissionaire's wife, who did the charing[1], and I gave her the order for the coffee.

'I wrote two more articles, and then, feeling more drowsy than ever, I rose and walked up and down the room to stretch my legs. My coffee had not yet come, and I wondered what the cause of the delay[2] could be. Opening the door, I started down the corridor to find out. There was a straight passage dimly lit[3] which led from the room in which I had been working, and was the only exit from it. It ended in a curving staircase[4], with the commissionaire's lodge in the passage at the bottom. Half-way down this staircase is a small landing[5], with another passage running into it[6] at right angles. The second one leads, by means of[7] a second small stair, to a side-door[8] used by servants, and also as a short cut[9] by clerks when coming from Charles Street.

'Here is a rough[10] chart[11] of the place.'

'Thank you. I think that I quite follow you,' said Sherlock Holmes.

'It is of the utmost importance that you should notice this point. I went down the stairs and into the hall, where I found the commissionaire fast asleep in his box, with the kettle[12] boiling furiously upon the spirit-lamp, for the water was spurting[13] over the floor. I had put out[14] my hand and was about[15] to shake the man, who was still sleeping soundly[16], when a bell over his head rang loudly, and he woke with a start[17].

' "Mr. Phelps, sir!" said he, looking at me in bewilderment[18].

' "I came down to see if my coffee was ready."

' "I was boiling the kettle when I fell asleep, sir."

He looked at me and then up at the still quivering bell[19], with an ever-growing[20] astonishment upon his face.

1. ménage
2. retard
3. mal éclairé
4. escalier en colimaçon
5. palier
6. qui le coupe
7. par
8. porte latérale
9. raccourci
10. sommaire
11. plan
12. bouilloire
13. giclait
14. tendu
15. m'apprêtais
16. à poings fermés
17. en sursaut
18. ébahi
19. sonnette qui tressautait encore
20. grandissant

' "If you was here, sir, then who rang the bell?" he asked.

' "The bell!" I said. "What bell is it?"

' "It's the bell of the room you were working in."

'A cold hand seemed to close round my heart. Someone, then, was in that room where my precious treaty lay upon the table. I ran frantically[1] up the stairs and along the passage. There was no one in the corridor, Mr. Holmes. There was no one in the room. All was exactly as I left it, save only that[2] the papers committed to my care[3] had been taken from the desk on which they lay. The copy was there and the original was gone.'

Holmes sat up in his chair and rubbed his hands. I could see that the problem was entirely to his heart[4]. 'Pray, what did you do then?' he murmured.

'I recognized in an instant that the thief must have come up the stairs from the side-door. Of course I must have met him[5] if he had come the other way.'

'You were satisfied[6] that he could not have been concealed[7] in the room all the time, or in the corridor which you have just described as dimly lighted?'

'It is absolutely impossible. A rat could not conceal himself either in the room or the corridor. There is no cover at all[8].'

'Thank you. Pray proceed[9].'

'The commissionaire, seeing by my pale face that something was to be feared, had followed me upstairs. Now we both rushed along the corridor and down the steep steps[10] which led to Charles Street. The door at the bottom was closed but unlocked[11]. We flung it open and rushed out. I can distinctly remember that as we did so there came three chimes from[12] a neighbouring[13] church. It was a quarter to ten.'

1. comme un fou
2. à ceci près que
3. qui m'avaient été confiés
4. de ceux qu'il chérissait
5. Je l'aurais nécessairement croisé
6. convaincu
7. se cacher
8. nulle part où se cacher
9. Poursuivez, je vous prie
10. hautes marches
11. déverrouillée
12. trois coups ont sonné à
13. avoisinante

'That is of enormous importance,' said Holmes, making a note upon his shirt cuff[1].

'The night was very dark, and a thin, warm rain was falling. There was no one in Charles Street, but a great traffic was going on, as usual, in Whitehall, at the extremity. We rushed along the pavement, bareheaded as we were[2], and at the far corner we found a policeman standing.

' "A robbery[3] has been committed," I gasped[4]. "A document of immense value has been stolen from the Foreign Office. Has anyone passed this way?'

' "I have been standing here for a quarter of an hour, sir," said he; "only one person has passed during that time – a woman, tall and elderly, with a Paisley shawl[5]."

' "Ah, that is only my wife," cried the commissionaire. "Has no one else passed?"

' "No one."

' "Then it must be the other way that the thief took," cried the fellow, tugging at my sleeve[6].

'But I was not satisfied, and the attempts which he made to draw me away[7] increased my suspicions.

' "Which way did the woman go?" I cried.

' "I don't know, sir. I noticed her pass, but I had no special reason for watching her. She seemed to be in a hurry."

' "How long ago was it?"

' "Oh, not very many minutes."

' "Within the last five?"

' "Well, it could not be more than five."

' "You're only wasting your time, sir, and every minute now is of importance," cried the commissionaire. "Take my word for it that[8] my old woman has nothing to do with it, and come down to the other end of the street. Well, if you won't, I will," and with that he rushed off in the other direction.

1. manchette
2. tête nue
3. vol
4. me suis-je écrié, haletant
5. châle à impression cachemire
6. en me tirant par la manche
7. m'éloigner
8. Croyez-moi,

'But I was after him in an instant and caught him by the sleeve.

' "Where do you live?" said I.

' " No. 16, Ivy Lane, Brixton," he answered; "but don't let yourself be drawn away[1] upon a false scent[2], Mr. Phelps. Come to the other end of the street, and let us see if we can hear[3] of anything."

'Nothing was to be lost[4] by following his advice. With the policeman we both hurried down, but only to find the street full of traffic, many people coming and going, but all only too eager[5] to get to a place of safety[6] upon so wet a night. There was no lounger[7] who could tell us who had passed.

'Then we returned to the office, and searched the stairs and the passage without result. The corridor which led to the room was laid down[8] with a kind of creamy[9] linoleum, which shows an impression very easily[10]. We examined it very carefully, but found no outline of any footmark[11].'

'Had it been raining all the evening?'

'Since about seven.'

'How is it, then, that the woman who came into the room about nine left no traces with her muddy[12] boots?'

'I am glad you raise the point[13]. It occurred to me[14] at the time. The charwomen[15] are in the habit[16] of taking off their boots at the commissionaire's office, and putting on list slippers[17].'

'That is very clear. There were no marks, then, though the night was a wet one? The chain[18] of events is certainly one of extraordinary interest. What did you do next?'

'We examined the room also. There was no possibility of a secret door, and the windows are quite[19] thirty feet[20] from the ground. Both of them were fastened[21] on the inside. The carpet prevents[22] any

1. embarquer
2. piste
3. avoir vent
4. On ne perdrait rien
5. s'empressant
6. d'aller se mettre à l'abri
7. flâneur
8. recouvert
9. de couleur crème
10. où les traces restent très visibles
11. empreinte de pas
12. couvertes de boue
13. que vous évoquiez la question
14. Je me la suis posée
15. femmes de ménage
16. ont pour habitude
17. des chaussons [de lisière]
18. enchaînement
19. bien à
20. plus de 9 m
21. fermées
22. écarte

possibility of a trap-door[1], and the ceiling is of the ordinary whitewashed[2] kind. I will pledge my life[3] that whoever[4] stole my papers could only have come through the door.'

'How about the fireplace[5]?'

'They use none. There is a stove[6]. The bell-rope[7] hangs from the wire[8] just to the right of my desk. Whoever rang it must have come right up to the desk to do it. But why should any criminal wish to ring the bell? It is a most insoluble mystery.'

'Certainly the incident was unusual. What were your next steps[9]? You examined the room, I presume, to see if the intruder[10] had left any traces – any cigar-end, or dropped glove, or hair-pin, or other trifle[11]?'

'There was nothing of the sort.'

'No smell?'

'Well, we never thought of that.'

'Ah, a scent of tobacco would have been worth a great deal to us[12] in such an investigation.'

'I never smoke myself, so I think I should have observed it if there had been any smell of tobacco. There was absolutely no clue[13] of any kind. The only[14] tangible fact was that the commissionaire's wife – Mrs. Tangey was the name – had hurried out of the place. He could give no explanation save that it was about the time when the woman always went home. The policeman and I agreed that our best plan would be to seize the woman before she could get rid of the papers, presuming that she had them.

'The alarm had reached Scotland Yard by this time, and Mr. Forbes, the detective[15], came round at once and took up the case[16] with a great deal of energy. We hired a hansom[17], and in half an hour we were at the address which had been given to us. A young woman opened the door, who proved to be[18]

1. trappe
2. blanchi à la chaux
3. jurerais sur ma vie
4. quiconque
5. cheminée
6. un poêle
7. cordon de la sonnette
8. câble
9. Qu'avez-vous fait ensuite
10. intrus
11. bricole
12. nous aurait été d'un grand secours
13. indice
14. seul
15. inspecteur
16. s'est saisi de l'affaire
17. fiacre
18. s'est avéré être

Mrs. Tangey's eldest daughter. Her mother had not come back yet, and we were shown into the front room to wait.

'About ten minutes later a knock came at the door, and here we made the one[1] serious mistake for which I blame myself. Instead of opening the door ourselves we allowed the girl to do so. We heard her say, "Mother, there are two men in the house waiting to see you," and an instant afterwards we heard the patter of feet rushing down the passage[2]. Forbes flung open the door[3], and we both ran into the back room or kitchen, but the woman had got there before us. She stared at us with defiant eyes[4], and then suddenly recognizing me, an expression of absolute astonishment came over her face.

' "Why, if it isn't[5] Mr. Phelps, of the office!" she cried.

' "Come[6], come, who did you think we were when you ran away from us?" asked my companion.

' "I thought you were the brokers[7]," said she. "We've had some trouble with a tradesman[8]."

' "That's not quite good enough," answered Forbes.

"We have reason to believe that you have taken a paper of importance from the Foreign Office, and that you ran in here to dispose of it[9]. You must come back with us to Scotland Yard to be searched[10]."

'It was in vain that she protested and resisted. A four-wheeler[11] was brought, and we all three drove back in it. We had first made an examination of the kitchen, and especially of the kitchen fire, to see whether she might have made away with[12] the papers during the instant that she was alone. There were no signs, however, of any ashes or scraps[13]. When we reached Scotland Yard she was handed over at once to the female searcher[14]. I waited in an

1. seule
2. un bruit de pas précipités dans le couloir
3. a ouvert la porte à toute volée
4. d'un air de défi
5. Çà alors, mais c'est
6. Allons
7. revendeurs
8. commerçant
9. vous en débarrasser
10. fouillée
11. fiacre
12. si elle n'avait pas détruit
13. fragments
14. la préposée à la fouille

agony of suspense[1] until she came back with her report. There were no signs of the papers.

'Then, for the first time, the horror of my situation came in its full force upon me[2]. Hitherto[3] I had been acting, and action had numbed[4] thought. I had been so confident[5] of regaining the treaty at once that I had not dared to think of what would be the consequence if I failed to do so. But now there was nothing more to be done, and I had leisure to[6] realize my position. It was horrible! Watson there would tell you that I was a nervous, sensitive[7] boy at school. It is my nature. I thought of my uncle and of his colleagues in the Cabinet, of the shame[8] which I had brought upon him, upon myself, upon everyone connected with me. What though[9] I was the victim of an extraordinary accident? No allowance is made for[10] accidents where[11] diplomatic interests are at stake[12]. I was ruined; shamefully, hopelessly[13] ruined. I don't know what I did. I fancy I must have made a scene. I have a dim recollection[14] of a group of officials who crowded[15] round me endeavouring[16] to soothe me[17]. One of them drove down with me to Waterloo and saw me into the[18] Woking train. I believe that he would have come all the way had it not been that[19] Dr. Ferrier, who lives near me, was going down by that very[20] train. The doctor most kindly took charge of me, and it was well he did so, for[21] I had a fit[22] in the station, and before we reached home I was practically a raving maniac[23].

'You can imagine the state of things[24] here when they were roused from[25] their beds by the doctor's ringing, and found me in this condition[26]. Poor Annie here and my mother were broken-hearted. Dr. Ferrier had just heard enough from the detective[27] at the station to be able to give an idea of

1. fou d'impatience
2. la situation m'est apparue dans toute son horreur
3. Jusqu'alors
4. paralysé
5. sûr
6. tout loisir de
7. sensible
8. la honte
9. Et même si
10. On ne fait preuve d'aucune indulgence en cas d'
11. quand
12. en jeu
13. irrémédiablement
14. le vague souvenir
15. se sont attroupés
16. en s'efforçant
17. de m'apaiser
18. m'a accompagné jusqu'au
19. s'il n'y avait pas eu
20. et qui descendait par le même
21. car
22. crise de nerfs
23. en plein délire
24. situation
25. tirés de
26. état
27. inspecteur

1. n'a pas arrangé les affaires
2. j'allais connaître
3. délogé
4. riante
5. en proie à des délires
6. dus à la fièvre cérébrale
7. Sans
8. sans
9. pendant la journée
10. infirmière rétribuée
11. s'est rétablie
12. télégraphier
13. s'est attardé
14. Cette prolongation
15. origine
16. l'affaire n'a pas eu de suite
17. ne me venez pas en aide
18. mon poste
19. perdus à jamais
20. malade
21. discours
22. remède

what had happened, and his story did not mend matters[1]. It was evident to all that I was in for[2] a long illness, so Joseph was bundled out[3] of this cheery[4] bedroom, and it was turned into a sick-room for me. Here I have lain, Mr. Holmes, for over nine weeks, unconscious, and raving[5] with brain fever[6]. If it had not been for[7] Miss Harrison here and for[8] the doctor's care I should not be speaking to you now. She has nursed me by day[9], and a hired nurse[10] has looked after me by night, for in my mad fits I was capable of anything. Slowly my reason has cleared[11], but it is only during the last three days that my memory has quite returned. Sometimes I wish that it never had. The first thing I did was to wire[12] to Mr. Forbes, who had the case in hand. He came out and assured me that, though everything has been done, no trace of a clue has been discovered. The commissionaire and his wife have been examined in every way without any light being thrown upon the matter. The suspicions of the police then rested upon young Gorot, who, as you may remember, stayed overtime[13] in the office that night. His remaining behind[14] and his French name were really the only two points which could suggest suspicion; but as a matter of fact, I did not begin work until he had gone, and his people are of Huguenot extraction[15], but as English in sympathy and tradition as you and I are. Nothing was found to implicate him in any way, and there the matter dropped[16]. I turn to you, Mr. Holmes, as absolutely my last hope. If you fail me[17], then my honour as well as my position[18] are for ever forfeited[19].'

The invalid[20] sank back upon his cushions, tired out by this long recital[21], while his nurse poured him out a glass of some stimulating medicine[22]. Holmes sat silently with his head thrown back and his eyes closed in an attitude which might seem listless[1] to a stranger, but which I knew betokened[2] the most intense absorption[3].

'Your statement[4] has been so explicit,' said he at last, 'that you have really left me very few questions to ask. There is one of the very utmost importance, however. Did you tell anyone that you had this special task to perform?'

'No one.'

'Not Miss Harrison here, for example?'

'No. I had not been back to Woking between getting the order and executing the commission.'

'And none of your people[5] had by chance[6] been to see you?'

'None.'

'Did any of them know their way about[7] in the office?'

'Oh, yes; all of them had been shown over it[8].'

'Still, of course, if you said nothing to anyone about the treaty, these inquiries are irrelevant[9].'

'I said nothing.'

'Do you know anything of the commissionaire?'

'Nothing, except that he is an old soldier.'

'What regiment?'

'Oh, I have heard – Coldstream Guards.'

'Thank you. I have no doubt I can get details from Forbes. The authorities are excellent at amassing facts, though they do not always use them to advantage. What a lovely thing a rose is!'

He walked past the couch[10] to the open window, and held up the drooping stalk[11] of a moss rose[12], looking down at the dainty[13] blend[14] of crimson[15] and green. It was a new phase[16] of his character to me, for I had never before seen him show any keen[17] interest in natural objects.

1. indolente
2. dénotait
3. concentration
4. exposé
5. personne de votre famille
6. par hasard
7. la disposition des lieux
8. on le leur avait fait voir à tous
9. hors de propos
10. canapé
11. tige affaissée
12. de rosier mousseux
13. délicate
14. association
15. pourpre
16. aspect
17. vif

'There is nothing in which deduction is so necessary as in religion,' said he, leaning with his back against the shutters[1]. 'It can be built up as an exact science by the reasoner[2]. Our highest assurance of the goodness of Providence seems to me to rest in[3] the flowers. All other things, our powers, our desires, our food, are really necessary for our existence in the first instance[4]. But this rose is an extra[5]. Its smell and its colour are an embellishment of life, not a condition of it. It is only goodness which gives extras, and so I say again that we have much to hope from the flowers.'

Percy Phelps and his nurse looked at Holmes during this demonstration with surprise and a good deal of disappointment written upon their faces. He had fallen into a reverie, with the moss rose between his fingers. It had lasted some minutes[6] before the young lady broke in upon it[7].

'Do you see any prospect[8] of solving[9] this mystery, Mr. Holmes?' she asked, with a touch of asperity in her voice[10].

'Oh, the mystery!' he answered, coming back with a start[11] to the realities of life. 'Well, it would be absurd to deny that the case is a very abstruse[12] and complicated one; but I can promise you that I will look into the matter and let you know any points which may strike me.'

'Do you see any clue?'

'You have furnished me with seven[13], but of course I must test them before I can pronounce upon their value.'

'You suspect someone?'

'I suspect myself–'

'What?'

'Of coming to conclusions too rapidly.'

'Then go to London and test your conclusions!'

1. volets
2. penseur
3. être fournie par
4. des besoins de première nécessité
5. vient en supplément
6. Quelques minutes s'écoulèrent
7. ne l'interrompît
8. espoir
9. résoudre
10. d'un ton un peu acerbe
11. en sursaut
12. hermétique
13. m'en avez fourni sept

'Your advice is very excellent, Miss Harrison,' said Holmes, rising. 'I think, Watson, we cannot do better. Do not allow yourself to indulge in[1] false hopes, Mr. Phelps. The affair is a very tangled one[2]!'

'I shall be in a fever until I see you again,' cried the diplomatist.

'Well, I'll come out by the same train tomorrow, though it's more than likely[3] that my report will be a negative one!'

'God bless you for promising to come,' cried our client. 'It gives me fresh life to know that something is being done. By the way[4], I have had a letter from Lord Holdhurst.'

'Ha! What did he say?'

'He was cold, but not harsh[5]. I dare say my severe[6] illness prevented him from being that[7]. He repeated that the matter was of the utmost importance, and added that no steps[8] would be taken about my future – by which he means, of course, my dismissal[9] – until my health was restored[10] and I had an opportunity[11] of repairing[12] my misfortune.'

'Well, that was reasonable and considerate[13],' said Holmes. 'Come, Watson, for we have a good day's work before us in town.'

Mr. Joseph Harrison drove us down to the station, and we were soon whirling up[14] in a Portsmouth train. Holmes was sunk in profound thought, and hardly opened his mouth until we had passed Clapham Junction.

'It's a very cheering thing[15] to come into London by any of these lines which run high[16] and allow you to look down upon the houses like this.'

I thought he was joking, for the view was sordid enough[17], but he soon explained himself.

1. Ne vous laissez pas bercer de
2. très embrouillée
3. plus que probable
4. Au fait
5. dur
6. grave
7. l'en a empêché
8. aucune mesure
9. renvoi
10. tant que je n'aurai pas recouvré la santé
11. qu'une occasion ne se sera pas présentée
12. remédier à
13. attentionné
14. bientôt nous roulions à toute vapeur
15. réjouissant
16. qui passent en contre-haut
17. passablement sordide

1. groupes
2. toits d'ardoise
3. couleur de plomb
4. nouvelles écoles primaires [mises en place par une loi de 1870]
5. Des phares
6. Les fanaux
7. graines
8. jaillira
9. forcés
10. un vrai bourbier
11. de le sortir de là
12. brave fille
13. maître de forges
14. du côté du Northumberland
15. s'est fiancé avec elle
16. catastrophe
17. bien au chaud
18. Mes patients
19. assez sèchement
20. période la plus creuse

'Look at those big, isolated clumps[1] of buildings rising up above the slates[2], like brick islands in a lead-coloured[3] sea.'

'The Board schools[4].'

'Lighthouses[5], my boy! Beacons[6] of the future! Capsules, with hundreds of bright little seeds[7] in each, out of which will spring[8] the wiser, better England of the future. I suppose that man Phelps does not drink?'

'I should not think so.'

'Nor should I. But we are bound[9] to take every possibility into account. The poor devil has certainly got himself into very deep water[10], and it's a question whether we shall ever be able to get him ashore[11]. What did you think of Miss Harrison?'

'A girl of strong character.'

'Yes, but she is a good sort[12], or I am mistaken. She and her brother are the only children of an iron-master[13] somewhere up Northumberland way[14]. Phelps got engaged to her[15] when travelling last winter, and she came down to be introduced to his people, with her brother as escort. Then came the smash[16], and she stayed on to nurse her lover, while brother Joseph, finding himself pretty snug[17], stayed on too. I've been making a few independent inquiries, you see. But today must be a day of inquiries.'

'My practice[18]–' I began.

'Oh, if you find your own cases more interesting than mine–' said Holmes, with some asperity[19].

'I was going to say that my practice could get along very well for a day or two, since it is the slackest time[20] in the year.'

'Excellent,' said he, recovering his good humour. 'Then we'll look into this matter together. I think that we should begin by seeing Forbes. He can probably tell us all the details we want, until we know from what side the case is to be approached.'

'You said you had a clue.'

'Well, we have several, but we can only test their value by further inquiry. The most difficult crime to track is the one which is purposeless[1]. Now, this is not purposeless. Who is it that profits by it? There is the French Ambassador, there is the Russian, there is whoever[2] might sell it to either of these[3], and there is Lord Holdhurst.'

'Lord Holdhurst!'

'Well, it is just conceivable that a statesman might find himself in a position where he was not sorry to have such a document accidentally destroyed.'

'Not a statesman with the honourable record of Lord Holdhurst.'

'It is a possibility, and we cannot afford[4] to disregard it[5]. We shall see the noble lord today, and find out if he can tell us anything. Meanwhile, I have already set inquiries upon foot[6].'

'Already?'

'Yes, I sent wires from Woking station to every evening paper[7] in London. This advertisement[8] will appear in each of them.'

He handed over a sheet torn from the notebook. On it was scribbled[9] in pencil:

'£10 Reward[10]. – The number of the cab[11] which dropped a fare[12] at or about[13] the door of the Foreign Office in Charles Street, at a quarter to ten in the evening of May 23rd. Apply[14] 221B Baker Street.'

'You are confident[15] that the thief came in a cab?'

'If not, there is no harm done. But if Mr. Phelps is correct in stating[16] that there is no hiding-place either in the room or the corridors, then the person must have come from outside. If he came from

1. sans mobile
2. quiconque
3. à l'un ou à l'autre
4. nous permettre
5. de la négliger
6. lancé des demandes de renseignement
7. tous les journaux du soir
8. annonce
9. griffonné
10. Récompense de 10 livres sterling
11. fiacre [taxi hippomobile]
12. client
13. devant ou à proximité de
14. Se présenter
15. sûr
16. en affirmant

outside on so wet a night, and yet left no trace of damp upon the linoleum, which was examined within a few minutes of his passing, then it is exceedingly probable that he came in a cab. Yes, I think that we may safely deduce a cab.'

'It sounds plausible.'

'That is one of the clues of which I spoke. It may lead us to something. And then, of course, there is the bell – which is the most distinctive feature of the case[1]. Why should the bell ring? Was it the thief that did it out of bravado[2]? Or was it someone who was with the thief who did it in order to prevent[3] the crime? Or was it an accident? Or was it–?' He sank back into the state of intense and silent thought from which he had emerged, but it seemed to me, accustomed as I was to his every mood, that some new possibility had dawned suddenly upon him[4].

It was twenty-past three when we reached our terminus, and after a hasty luncheon[5] at the buffet we pushed on at once to Scotland Yard. Holmes had already wired to Forbes, and we found him waiting to receive us: a small, foxy[6] man, with a sharp but by no means[7] amiable expression. He was decidedly frigid in his manner to[8] us, especially when he heard the errand upon which we had come[9].

'I've heard of your methods before now, Mr. Holmes,' said he, tartly[10]. 'You are ready enough to use all the information that the police can lay at your disposal, and then you try to finish the case yourself and bring discredit upon them.'

'On the contrary,' said Holmes; 'out of[11] my last fifty-three cases my name has only appeared in four, and the police have had all the credit[12] in forty-nine. I don't blame you for not knowing this; for you are young and inexperienced; but if you

1. la particularité de cette affaire
2. par bravade
3. empêcher
4. lui était soudain apparue
5. déjeuner
6. rusé
7. tout sauf
8. très froid envers
9. la raison de notre venue
10. d'un ton aigre
11. sur
12. récolté tous les lauriers

wished to get on[1] in your new duties[2] you will work with me, and not against me.'

'I'd be very glad of a hint[3] or two,' said the detective, changing his manner. 'I've certainly had no credit from the case so far.'

'What steps have you taken?'

'Tangey, the commissionaire, has been shadowed[4]. He left the Guards with a good character[5], and we can find nothing against him. His wife is a bad lot[6], though. I fancy she knows more about this than appears.'

'Have you shadowed her?'

'We have set one of our women on to her. Mrs. Tangey drinks, and our woman has been with her twice when she was well on[7], but she could get nothing out of her.'

'I understand that they have had brokers[8] in the house?

'Yes, but they were paid off.'

'Where did the money come from?'

'That was all right. His pension was due[9]; they have not shown any sign of being in funds[10].'

'What explanation did she give of having answered the bell when Mr. Phelps rang for the coffee?'

'She said that her husband was very tired and she wished to relieve him[11].'

'Well, certainly that would agree[12] with his being found, a little later, asleep in his chair. There is nothing against them, then, but[13] the woman's character. Did you ask her why she hurried away that night? Her haste attracted the attention of the police-constable[14].'

'She was later than usual, and wanted to get home.

1. faire votre chemin
2. fonctions,
3. suggestion
4. pris en filature
5. réputation
6. mauvaise graine
7. bien éméchée
8. revendeurs
9. Il allait toucher sa retraite
10. d'être particulièrement bien en fonds
11. le soulager
12. concorde
13. à part
14. l'agent de police

'Did you point out to her[1] that you and Mr. Phelps, who started at least twenty minutes after her, got there before her?'

'She explains that by the difference between a bus and a hansom.'

'Did she make it clear[2] why, on reaching her house, she ran into the back kitchen?'

'Because she had the money there with which to pay off the brokers.'

'She has at least an answer for everything. Did you ask her whether in leaving she met anyone or saw anyone loitering about[3] Charles Street?'

'She saw no one but[4] the constable.'

'Well, you seem to have cross-examined her pretty thoroughly[5]. What else have you done?'

'The clerk, Gorot, has been shadowed all these nine weeks, but without result. We can show nothing against him.'

'Anything else?'

'Well, we have nothing else to go upon[6] – no evidence of any kind[7].'

'Have you formed any theory about how that bell rang?'

'Well, I must confess that it beats me[8]. It was a cool hand[9], whoever it was, to go and give[10] the alarm like that.'

'Yes, it was a queer thing to do. Many thanks to you for what you have told me. If I can put the man into your hands you shall hear from me[11]. Come along, Watson!'

'Where are we going to now?' I asked, as we left the office.

'We are now going to interview Lord Holdhurst, the Cabinet Minister and future Premier[12] of England.'

1. Lui avez-vous fait remarquer
2. A-t-elle expliqué
3. traînant du côté de
4. à part
5. l'avoir soumise à un interrogatoire très serré
6. aucune autre piste
7. aucun indice quel qu'il soit
8. je n'en ai pas la moindre idée
9. Il ne manquait pas de sang-froid
10. celui qui a donné
11. je vous ferai signe
12. Premier ministre

We were fortunate[1] in finding[2] that Lord Holdhurst was still in his chambers at Downing Street, and on Holmes sending in[3] his card we were instantly shown up[4]. The statesman received us with that old-fashioned courtesy for which he is remarkable[5], and seated us on the two luxurious[6] easy chairs[7] on either side of the fireplace. Standing on the rug between us, with his slight, tall figure[8], his sharp-featured[9], thoughtful[10] face, and his curling hair prematurely tinged with grey[11], he seemed to represent that not too common type, a nobleman who is in truth noble[12].

'Your name is very familiar to me, Mr. Holmes,' said he, smiling. 'And, of course, I cannot pretend to be ignorant of the object of your visit. There has only been one occurrence[13] in these offices which could call for[14] your attention. In whose interest are you acting, may I ask?

'In that of Mr. Percy Phelps,' answered Holmes.

'Ah, my unfortunate nephew! You can understand that our kinship[15] makes it the more impossible for me to screen him[16] in any way. I fear that the incident must have a very prejudicial effect upon his career.'

'But if the document is found?'

'Ah, that, of course, would be different.'

'I had one or two questions which I wished to ask you, Lord Holdhurst.'

'I shall be happy to give you any information in my power.'

'Was it in this room that you gave your instructions as to[17] the copying of the document?'

'It was.'

'Then you could hardly[18] have been overheard?'

'It is out of the question.'

1. eûmes la chance
2. de constater
3. quand Holmes eut fait porter
4. introduits auprès de lui
5. qu'on lui connaît
6. luxueux
7. fauteuils
8. haute taille mince
9. anguleux
10. pensif
11. grisonnant
12. un gentilhomme qui en est vraiment un
13. événement
14. nécessiterait
15. parenté
16. le couvrir
17. relatives à
18. difficilement

'Did you ever mention to anyone that it was your intention to give out the treaty to be copied?'

'Never.'

'You are certain of that?'

'Absolutely.'

'Well, since you never said so, and Mr. Phelps never said so, and nobody else knew anything of the matter, then the thief's presence in the room was purely accidental. He saw his chance[1] and he took it[2].'

The statesman smiled. 'You take me out of my province there[3],' said he.

Holmes considered[4] for a moment. 'There is another very important point which I wish to discuss with you,' said he. 'You feared, as I understand, that very grave results might follow from[5] the details of this treaty becoming known[6]?'

A shadow passed over the expressive face of the statesman. 'Very grave results, indeed.'

'And have they occurred?'

'Not yet.'

'If the treaty had reached, let us say, the French or Russian Foreign Office, you would expect to hear of it?'

'I should,' said Lord Holdhurst, with a wry face[7].

'Since nearly ten weeks have elapsed[8], then, and nothing has been heard, it is not unfair[9] to suppose that for some reason the treaty has not reached them?'

Lord Holdhurst shrugged his[10] shoulders.

'We can hardly suppose, Mr. Holmes, that the thief took the treaty in order to frame it[11] and hang it up.'

'Perhaps he is waiting for a better price.'

1. L'occasion s'est présentée
2. s'en est saisi
3. Cela est hors de mon domaine
4. réfléchit
5. si
6. venaient à être connus
7. grimace
8. se sont écoulées
9. abusif
10. haussa les
11. l'encadrer

'If he waits a little longer he will get no price at all. The treaty will cease to be a secret in a few months.'

'That is most important,' said Holmes. 'Of course it is a possible supposition that the thief has had a sudden illness–'

'An attack of brain fever, for example?' asked the statesman, flashing a swift glance at him[1].

'I did not say so,' said Holmes, imperturbably. 'And now, Lord Holdhurst, we have already taken up too much of your valuable[2] time, and we shall wish you good day.'

'Every success to your investigation[3], be the criminal who it may[4],' answered the nobleman, as he bowed us out at the door[5].

'He's a fine fellow,' said Holmes, as we came out into Whitehall. 'But he has a struggle[6] to keep up his position[7]. He is far from rich, and has many calls[8]. You noticed, of course, that his boots had been re-soled[9]? Now, Watson, I won't detain you from your legitimate work any longer. I shall do nothing more today, unless I have an answer to my cab advertisement. But I should be extremely obliged to you if you would come down with me to Woking tomorrow, by the same train which we took today.'

I met him accordingly[10] next morning, and we travelled down to Woking together. He had had no answer to his advertisement, he said, and no fresh light had been thrown upon the case[11]. He had, when he so willed it[12], the utter immobility of countenance[13] of a Red Indian, and I could not gather[14] from his appearance whether he was satisfied or not with the position of the case[15]. His conversation, I remember, was about the Bertillon system of measurements[16], and he expressed his enthusiastic admiration of the French savant.

1. en lui lançant un coup d'œil

2. précieux

3. Je vous souhaite un succès plein et entier dans votre enquête

4. quel que soit le malfaiteur

5. en nous saluant sur le seuil

6. doit se débattre

7. garder son rang

8. obligations

9. ressemelées

10. donc

11. rien n'était venu nous éclairer

12. le voulait ainsi

13. totale impassibilité

14. déduire

15. avancement de l'affaire

16. mensurations [technique d'anthropométrie judiciaire]

We found our client still under the charge of his devoted nurse, but looking considerably better than before. He rose from the sofa and greeted us without difficulty when we entered.

'Any news?' he asked, eagerly[1].

'My report, as I expected, is a negative one,' said Holmes. 'I have seen Forbes, and I have seen your uncle, and I have set one or two trains of inquiry upon foot[2] which may lead to something.'

'You have not lost heart[3], then?'

'By no means[4].'

'God bless you for saying that!' cried Miss Harrison. 'If we keep our courage and our patience, the truth must come out.'

'We have more to tell you than you have for us,' said Phelps, re-seating himself upon the couch.

'I hoped you might have something.'

'Yes, we have had an adventure during the night, and one which might have proved to be a serious one.' His expression grew very grave as he spoke, and a look of something akin to[5] fear sprang up in his eyes. 'Do you know,' said he, 'that I begin to believe that I am the unconscious centre of some monstrous conspiracy, and that my life is aimed at[6] as well as my honour?'

'Ah!' cried Holmes.

'It sounds incredible, for I have not, as far as I know, an enemy in the world. Yet from last night's experience I can come to no other conclusion.'

'Pray let me hear it.'

'You must know that last night was the very[7] first night that I have ever slept without a nurse in the room. I was so much better that I thought I could dispense with one[8]. I had a night-light[9] burning, however. Well, about two in the morning I had sunk into a light sleep, when I was suddenly aroused[10] by

1. vivement
2. lancé une ou deux investigations
3. n'êtes pas découragé
4. Absolument pas
5. proche de
6. l'on en veut à ma vie
7. toute
8. m'en dispenser
9. veilleuse
10. réveillé

a slight noise. It was like the sound which a mouse makes when it is gnawing[1] a plank, and I lay listening to it for some time under the impression that it must come from that cause. Then it grew louder, and suddenly there came from the window a sharp metallic snick[2]. I sat up in amazement. There could be no doubt what the sounds were now. The faint[3] ones had been caused by someone forcing an instrument through the slit[4] between the sashes[5], and the second by the catch being pressed back[6].

There was a pause then for about ten minutes, as if the person were waiting to see whether the noise had awoken me. Then I heard a gentle creaking[7] as the window was very slowly opened. I could stand it no longer[8], for my nerves are not what they used to be. I sprang out of bed and flung open the shutters. A man was crouching[9] at the window. I could see little of him, for he was gone like a flash[10]. He was wrapped[11] in some sort of cloak[12], which came across the lower part of his face. One thing only I am sure of, and that is that he had some weapon[13] in his hand. It looked to me like a long knife. I distinctly saw the gleam[14] of it as he turned to run.'

'This is most interesting,' said Holmes. 'Pray[15], what did you do then?'

'I should have followed him through the open window if I had been stronger. As it was[16], I rang the bell and roused[17] the house. It took me some little time[18], for the bell rings in the kitchen, and the servants all sleep upstairs. I shouted, however, and that brought Joseph down, and he roused the others. Joseph and the groom found marks on the flower-bed[19] outside the window, but the weather has been so dry lately that they found it hopeless to follow the trail across the grass. There's a place,

1. en rongeant
2. clic très net
3. légers
4. fente
5. sur le châssis
6. lorsque le taquet avait été rabattu
7. grincement
8. Cela m'est devenu insupportable
9. accroupi
10. éclair
11. emmitouflé
12. cape
13. une arme
14. lueur
15. Dites-moi, je vous prie
16. En la circonstance
17. j'ai réveillé
18. un certain temps
19. plate-bande

however, on the wooden fence which skirts[1] the road which shows signs, they tell me, as if someone had got over and had snapped[2] the top of the rail in doing so. I have said nothing to the local police yet, for I thought I had best have your opinion first.'

This tale of our client's appeared to have an extraordinary effect upon Sherlock Holmes. He rose from his chair and paced about[3] the room in uncontrollable excitement.

'Misfortunes never come singly[4],' said Phelps, smiling, though it was evident that his adventure had somewhat shaken him.

'You have certainly had your share[5],' said Holmes. 'Do you think you could walk round the house with me?'

'Oh, yes, I should like a little sunshine. Joseph will come too.'

'And I also,' said Miss Harrison.

'I am afraid not,' said Holmes, shaking his head. 'I think I must ask you to remain sitting exactly where you are.'

The young lady resumed her seat[6] with an air of displeasure. Her brother, however, had joined us, and we set off[7] all four together. We passed round the lawn[8] to the outside of the young diplomatist's window. There were, as he had said, marks upon the flower-bed, but they were hopelessly blurred[9] and vague. Holmes stooped[10] over them for an instant, and then rose, shrugging his shoulders.

'I don't think anyone could make much of this[11],' said he. 'Let us go round the house and see why this particular room was chosen by the burglar[12]. I should have thought those larger windows of the drawing-room and dining-room would have had more attractions for him[13].'

1. qui longe
2. cassé net
3. se mit à arpenter
4. Un malheur n'arrive jamais seul
5. lot
6. se rassit
7. partîmes
8. contournâmes la pelouse
9. totalement floues
10. se pencha
11. en tirer grand-chose
12. cambrioleur
13. auraient plus suscité son intérêt

'They are more visible from the road,' suggested Mr. Joseph Harrison.

'Ah, yes, of course. There is a door here which he might have attempted. What is it for?'

'It is the side entrance for tradespeople[1]. Of course, it is locked at night!'

'Have you ever had an alarm like this before?'

'Never,' said our client.

'Do you keep plate[2] in the house, or anything to attract burglars?'

'Nothing of value.'

Holmes strolled round[3] the house with his hands in his pockets, and a negligent[4] air which was unusual with him.

'By the way,' said he, to Joseph Harrison, 'you found some place, I understand, where the fellow scaled the fence[5]. Let us have a look at that.'

The plump young man led us to a spot where the top of one of the wooden rails had been cracked. A small fragment of the wood was hanging down. Holmes pulled it off and examined it critically[6].

'Do you think that was done last night? It looks rather old, does it not?'

'Well, possibly so.'

'There are no marks of anyone jumping down upon the other side. No, I fancy we shall get no help here. Let us go back to the bedroom and talk the matter over[7].'

Percy Phelps was walking very slowly, leaning upon the arm of his future brother-in-law. Holmes walked swiftly across the lawn, and we were at the open window of the bedroom long before the others came up.

'Miss Harrison,' said Holmes, speaking with the utmost intensity of manner[8]. 'You must stay where you are all day. Let nothing prevent you[9] from

1. les fournisseurs

2. de l'argenterie

3. déambula dans

4. nonchalant

5. a écaillé la barrière

6. d'un œil critique

7. pour discuter de l'affaire

8. la plus grande véhémence

9. Que rien ne vous empêche

staying where you are all day. It is of the utmost importance.'

'Certainly, if you wish it, Mr. Holmes,' said the girl, in astonishment.

'When you go to bed lock the door of this room on the outside and keep the key. Promise to do this.'

'But Percy?'

'He will come to London with us.'

'And I am to remain here?'

'It is for his sake[1]. You can serve him[2]! Quick! Promise!'

She gave a nod of assent[3] just as the other two came up.

'Why do you sit moping there[4], Annie?' cried her brother. 'Come out into the sunshine!'

'No, thank you, Joseph. I have a slight headache[5], and this room is deliciously cool and soothing[6]!

'What do you propose now, Mr. Holmes?' asked our client.

'Well, in investigating this minor affair we must not lose sight of our main inquiry. It would be a very great help to me if you could come up to London with us.'

'At once?'

'Well, as soon as you conveniently[7] can. Say in an hour.'

'I feel quite strong enough, if I can really be of any help.'

'The greatest possible.'

'Perhaps you would like me to stay there to-night.'

'I was just going to propose it.'

'Then if my friend of the night comes to revisit me, he will find the bird flown. We are all in your hands, Mr. Holmes, and you must tell us exactly what you would like done. Perhaps you would

1. bien
2. lui rendre service
3. opina du chef
4. est-ce que tu restes assise là à te morfondre
5. mal de tête
6. apaisante
7. commodément

prefer that Joseph came with us, so as to look after me?'

'Oh, no; my friend Watson is a medical man, you know, and he'll look after you. We'll have our lunch here, if you will permit us, and then we shall all three set off for town together.'

It was arranged as he suggested, though Miss Harrison excused herself from leaving[1] the bedroom, in accordance with[2] Holmes's suggestion. What the object of my friend's manoeuvres was I could not conceive[3], unless it were to keep the lady away from Phelps, who, rejoiced by his returning health[4] and by the prospect[5] of action, lunched with us in the dining-room. Holmes had a still more startling surprise for us[6], however, for after accompanying us down to the station and seeing us into our carriage[7], he calmly announced that he had no intention of leaving Woking.

'There are one or two small points which I should desire to clear up[8] before I go,' said he. 'Your absence, Mr. Phelps, will in some ways rather assist me[9]. Watson, when you reach London you would oblige me by driving at once to Baker Street with our friend here, and remaining with him until I see you again. It is fortunate[10] that you are old schoolfellows, as you must have much to talk over. Mr. Phelps can have the spare bedroom[11] to-night, and I shall be with you in time for breakfast, for there is a train which will take me into Waterloo at eight.'

'But how about our investigation in London?' asked Phelps, ruefully[12].

'We can do that tomorrow. I think that just at present I can be of more immediate use here.'

1. demanda à ne pas quitter
2. conformément à
3. l'imaginer
4. d'avoir recouvré la santé
5. perspective
6. nous surprit encore davantage
7. compartiment
8. éclaircir
9. va m'être plutôt utile
10. heureux
11. chambre d'amis
12. d'un ton chagrin

'You might tell them at Briarbrae that I hope to be back tomorrow night,' cried Phelps, as we began to move from the platform[1].

'I hardly expect to go back to Briarbrae,' answered Holmes, and waved his hand to us cheerily[2] as we shot out from the station.

Phelps and I talked it over[3] on our journey[4], but neither of us could devise[5] a satisfactory reason for this new development[6].

'I suppose he wants to find out some clue as to the burglary[7] last night, if a burglar it was. For myself[8], I don't believe it was an ordinary thief.'

'What is your idea, then?'

'Upon my word[9], you may put it down to[10] my weak nerves or not, but I believe there is some deep political intrigue going on around me, and that, for some reason that passes my understanding[11], my life is aimed at by the conspirators[12]. It sounds high-flown[13] and absurd, but consider the facts! Why should a thief try to break in at[14] a bedroom window, where there could be no hope of any plunder[15], and why should he come with a long knife in his hand?'

'You are sure it was not a housebreaker's jemmy[16]?'

'Oh, no; it was a knife. I saw the flash of the blade quite distinctly.'

'But why on earth[17] should you be pursued with such animosity?'

'Ah! that is the question.'

'Well, if Holmes takes the same view[18], that would account for[19] his action, would it not? Presuming[20] that your theory is correct, if he can lay his hands upon the man who threatened you last night, he will have gone a long way towards finding[21] who took the naval treaty. It is absurd to

1. alors que le train s'ébranlait
2. gaiement
3. en discutâmes
4. durant le voyage
5. concevoir
6. rebondissement
7. concernant le cambriolage
8. Quant à moi
9. Ma parole
10. mettre ça sur le compte de
11. qui m'échappe
12. les conspirateurs en veulent à ma vie
13. excessif
14. de s'introduire par
15. butin
16. pince-monseigneur [levier]
17. diable
18. est du même avis
19. cela expliquerait
20. En supposant
21. sera bien plus près de découvrir

suppose that you have two enemies, one of whom robs you while the other threatens your life.'

'But Mr. Holmes said that he was not going to Briarbrae.'

'I have known him for some time,' said I, 'but I never knew him do anything yet without a very good reason,' and with that our conversation drifted off into[1] other topics[2].

But it was a weary[3] day for me. Phelps was still weak after his long illness, and his misfortunes made him querulous[4] and nervous. In vain I endeavoured[5] to interest him in Afghanistan, in India, in social questions, in anything which might take his mind out of the groove[6]. He would always come back to his lost treaty; wondering, guessing, speculating, as to what[7] Holmes was doing, what steps[8] Lord Holdhurst was taking, what news we should have in the morning. As the evening wore on[9] his excitement became quite painful.

'You have implicit faith in[10] Holmes?' he asked.

'I have seen him do some remarkable things.'

'But he never brought light into anything quite so dark as this?'

'Oh, yes; I have known him solve questions which presented fewer clues than yours.'

'But not where such large interests are at stake[11]?'

'I don't know that. To my certain knowledge he[12] has acted on behalf of[13] three of the reigning Houses of Europe in very vital matters.'

'But you know him well, Watson. He is such an inscrutable[14] fellow, that I never quite know what to make of him[15]. Do you think he is hopeful[16]? Do you think he expects to make a success of it[17]?'

'He has said nothing.'

'That is a bad sign.'

1. dériva vers
2. sujets
3. éreintant
4. grincheux
5. m'efforçai
6. lui changer les idées
7. se demandant ce que
8. mesures
9. avançait,
10. faites une confiance absolue à
11. en jeu
12. Je sais de façon certaine qu'il
13. pour le compte de
14. impénétrable
15. quoi penser de lui
16. garde espoir
17. compte réussir

'On the contrary, I have noticed that when he is off the trail[1] he generally says so. It is when he is on a scent, and is not quite absolutely sure yet that it is the right one, that he is most taciturn. Now, my dear fellow, we can't help matters by making ourselves nervous about them, so let me implore you to go to bed, and so be fresh for whatever may await us tomorrow.'

I was able at last to persuade my companion to take my advice, though I knew from his excited manner that there was not much hope of sleep for him. Indeed, his mood[2] was infectious[3], for I lay tossing[4] half the night myself, brooding over[5] this strange problem, and inventing a hundred theories, each of which was more impossible than the last[6]. Why had Holmes remained at Woking? Why had he asked Miss Harrison to stay in the sick-room all day? Why had he been so careful not to inform the people at Briarbrae that he intended to remain near them? I cudgelled my brains[7] until I fell asleep in the endeavour[8] to find some explanation which would cover all these facts.

It was seven o'clock when I awoke, and I set off at once for Phelps' room, to find him haggard and spent[9] after a sleepless night. His first question was whether Holmes had arrived yet.

'He'll be here when he promised,' said I, 'and not an instant sooner or later.'

And my words were true, for shortly after eight a hansom[10] dashed up to[11] the door and our friend got out of it. Standing in the window, we saw that his left hand was swathed[12] in a bandage and that his face was very grim and pale[13]. He entered the house, but it was some little time before he came upstairs.

'He looks like a beaten man[14],' cried Phelps.

1. a perdu la piste,
2. humeur
3. contagieuse
4. à me retourner dans mon lit
5. à ressasser
6. la précédente
7. me creusai les méninges
8. mes efforts
9. épuisé
10. fiacre
11. surgit devant
12. enveloppée
13. il était très pâle et faisait grise mine
14. vaincu

I was forced to confess that he was right. 'After all,' said I, 'the clue of the matter lies probably here in town.'

Phelps gave a groan[1].

'I don't know how it is[2],' said he, 'but I had hoped for so much from his return. But surely his hand was not tied up[3] like that yesterday? What can be the matter?'

'You are not wounded[4], Holmes?' I asked, as my friend entered the room.

'Tut[5], it is only a scratch[6] through[7] my own clumsiness[8],' he answered, nodding his good morning to us[9]. 'This case of yours, Mr. Phelps, is certainly one of the darkest which I have ever investigated.'

'I feared that you would find it beyond you[10].'

'It has been a most remarkable experience.'

'That bandage tells of[11] adventures,' said I. 'Won't you tell us what has happened?'

'After breakfast, my dear Watson. Remember that I have breathed thirty miles of Surrey air this morning. I suppose there has been no answer to my cabman advertisement? Well, well, we cannot expect to score[12] every time.'

The table was all laid[13], and, just as I was about to ring, Mrs. Hudson entered with the tea and coffee. A few minutes later she brought in the covers[14], and we all drew up to the table, Holmes ravenous[15], I curious, and Phelps in the gloomiest state of depression[16].

'Mrs. Hudson has risen to the occasion[17],' said Holmes, uncovering a dish of curried chicken. 'Her cuisine is a little limited, but she has as good an idea of breakfast as a Scotchwoman[18]. What have you there, Watson?'

'Ham and eggs,' I answered.

1. émit un grognement
2. cela se fait
3. bandée
4. blessé
5. Tss, tss
6. égratignure
7. due à
8. maladresse
9. en nous souhaitant le bonjour d'un signe de la tête
10. au-delà de vos compétences
11. suggère
12. réussir
13. mise
14. plats
15. affamé
16. dans un état de grand abattement
17. se montre à la hauteur des circonstances
18. son idée du petit déjeuner [complet] vaut bien celle d'une Écossaise

'Good! What are you going to take, Mr. Phelps: curried fowl[1], eggs, or will you help yourself[2]?'

'Thank you, I can eat nothing,' said Phelps.

'Oh, come[3]! Try the dish before you.'

'Thank you, I would really rather not.'

'Well, then,' said Holmes, with a mischievous[4] twinkle[5], 'I suppose that you have no objection to helping me[6]?'

Phelps raised the cover, and as he did so he uttered[7] a scream, and sat there staring[8] with a face as white as the plate upon which he looked. Across the centre of it was lying a little cylinder of blue-grey paper.

He caught it up, devoured it with his eyes, and then danced madly about[9] the room, pressing it to his bosom[10] and shrieking out in his delight[11]. Then he fell back into an arm-chair, so limp[12] and exhausted with his own emotions that we had to pour[13] brandy down his throat to keep him from fainting[14].

'There! there!' said Holmes, soothingly[15], patting him upon[16] the shoulder. 'It was too bad[17] to spring it on you[18] like this; but Watson here will tell you that I never can resist a touch of the dramatic[19].'

Phelps seized his hand and kissed it. 'God bless you!' he cried; 'you have saved my honour.'

'Well, my own was at stake, you know,' said Holmes. 'I assure you, it is just as hateful[20] to me to fail[21] in a case as it can be to you to blunder[22] over a commission[23].'

Phelps thrust away[24] the precious document into the innermost[25] pocket of his coat.

'I have not the heart to interrupt your breakfast any further, and yet I am dying to know how you got it and where it was.'

1. volaille au curry
2. je vous laisse vous servir
3. Allons, allons
4. malicieuse
5. lueur
6. me servir
7. poussa
8. le regard fixe
9. dans
10. contre lui
11. criant sa joie
12. faible
13. lui verser
14. l'empêcher de s'évanouir
15. sur un ton apaisant
16. en lui tapotant
17. déplorable
18. de vous surprendre
19. mise en scène
20. pénible
21. d'échouer
22. de faire une bourde
23. lors d'une mission
24. rangea à la hâte
25. la plus secrète

Sherlock Holmes swallowed a cup of coffee and turned his attention to the ham and eggs. Then he rose, lit his pipe, and settled himself down into his chair.

'I'll tell you what I did first, and how I came to do it[1] afterwards,' said he. 'After leaving you at the station I went for a charming walk through some admirable Surrey scenery[2] to a pretty little village called Ripley, where I had my tea at an inn[3], and took the precaution of filling my flask[4] and of putting a paper of sandwiches[5] in my pocket. There I remained until evening, when I set off for Woking again and found myself in the high-road outside Briarbrae just after sunset.

'Well, I waited until the road was clear[6] – it is never a very frequented one at any time, I fancy – and then I clambered[7] over the fence into the grounds.'

'Surely the gate was open?' ejaculated[8] Phelps.

'Yes; but I have a peculiar taste in these matters. I chose the place where the three fir trees[9] stand, and behind their screen[10] I got over without the least chance[11] of anyone in the house being able to see me. I crouched down[12] among the bushes on the other side, and crawled[13] from one to the other – witness the disreputable state[14] of my trouser knees – until I had reached the clump[15] of rhododendrons just opposite to your bedroom window. There I squatted down[16] and awaited developments[17].

'The blind[18] was not down in your room, and I could see Miss Harrison sitting there reading by the table. It was a quarter past ten when she closed her book, fastened the shutters[19], and retired. I heard her shut the door, and felt quite sure that she had turned the key in the lock.'

1. ce qui m'a poussé à le faire
2. paysage
3. auberge
4. gourde
5. un encas
6. soit libre
7. ai grimpé
8. s'écria
9. sapins
10. à couvert de ces arbres,
11. le moindre risque
12. me suis accroupi
13. ai rampé
14. voyez le triste état
15. massif
16. me suis tapi
17. la suite
18. store
19. a fermé les volets

1. s'écria
2. instructions
3. fastidieuse
4. veille
5. chasseur
6. proie
7. *Ruban tacheté*
8. verrou
9. grincement
10. en cas d'alerte
11. sur la pointe des pieds
12. a introduit
13. a défait le taquet
14. la fente entre les volets [avec la fenêtre à guillotine, les volets sont à l'intérieur de l'habitation]
15. a soulevé la barre

'The key?' ejaculated[1] Phelps.

'Yes, I had given Miss Harrison instructions to lock the door on the outside and take the key with her when she went to bed. She carried out every one of my injunctions[2] to the letter, and certainly without her co-operation you would not have that paper in your coat pocket. She departed then, the lights went out, and I was left squatting in the rhododendron bush.

'The night was fine, but still it was a very weary[3] vigil[4]. Of course, it has the sort of excitement about it that the sportsman[5] feels when he lies beside the watercourse and waits for the big game[6]. It was very long, though - almost as long, Watson, as when you and I waited in that deadly room when we looked into the little problem of the *Speckled Band*[7]. There was a church clock down at Woking which struck the quarters, and I thought more than once that it had stopped. At last, however, about two in the morning, I suddenly heard the gentle sound of a bolt[8] being pushed back, and the creaking[9] of a key. A moment later the servants' door was opened and Mr. Joseph Harrison stepped out into the moonlight.'

'Joseph!' ejaculated Phelps.

'He was bare-headed, but he had a black cloak thrown over his shoulder, so that he could conceal his face in an instant if there were any alarm[10]. He walked on tiptoe[11] under the shadow of the wall, and when he reached the window, he worked[12] a long-bladed knife through the sash and pushed back the catch[13]. Then he flung open the window and, putting his knife through the crack in the shutters[14], he thrust the bar up[15] and swung them open.

'From where I lay I had a perfect view of the inside of the room and of every one of his movements. He lit the two candles which stand upon the mantelpiece[1], and then he proceeded to[2] turn back the corner of the carpet in the neighbourhood[3] of the door. Presently he stooped and picked out[4] a square piece of board[5], such as is usually left to enable plumbers to get[6] at the joints[7] of the gas pipes[8]. This one covered, as a matter of fact, the T-joint[9] which gives off[10] the pipe which supplies[11] the kitchen underneath. Out of this hiding-place he drew that little cylinder of paper, pushed down the board, rearranged the carpet, blew out the candles, and walked straight into my arms as I stood waiting for him outside the window.

'Well, he has rather more viciousness[12] than I gave him credit for[13], has Master Joseph. He flew at me with his knife, and I had to grass him[14] twice, and got a cut over the knuckles[15], before I had the upper hand of him[16]. He looked murder[17] out of the only eye he could see with[18] when we had finished, but he listened to reason and gave up the papers. Having got them I let my man go, but I wired full particulars[19] to Forbes this morning. If he is quick enough to catch his bird, well and good[20]! But if, as I shrewdly suspect[21], he finds the nest empty before he gets there, why, all the better[22] for the Government. I fancy that Lord Holdhurst, for one[23], and Mr. Percy Phelps, for another[24], would very much rather[25] that the affair never got so far as a police-court[26].'

'My God!' gasped[27] our client. 'Do you tell me that during these long ten weeks of agony[28], the stolen papers were within the very room[29] with me all the time?'

'So it was.'

'And Joseph! Joseph a villain[30] and a thief!'

1. cheminée
2. s'est mis à
3. près
4. a dégagé
5. planchette carrée
6. d'accéder
7. raccords
8. tuyaux
9. raccord en T
10. d'où part
11. alimente
12. est encore plus mauvais
13. que je ne l'avais cru
14. l'envoyer à terre
15. sur les phalanges
16. j'aie le dessus
17. me regardait d'un air furieux
18. du seul œil valide qui lui restait
19. des informations complètes
20. fort bien
21. comme je le soupçonne fort
22. eh bien tant mieux
23. d'une part
24. d'autre part
25. préféreraient de loin
26. ne donne pas lieu à des poursuites
27. s'écria dans un souffle
28. angoisse
29. la chambre même
30. scélérat

'Hum! I am afraid Joseph's character is a rather deeper and more dangerous one than one might judge from his appearance. From what I have heard from him this morning, I gather that he has lost heavily in dabbling with stocks[1], and that he is ready to do anything on earth to better his fortunes[2]. Being an absolutely selfish[3] man, when a chance presented itself he did not allow either his sister's happiness or your reputation to hold his hand[4].'

Percy Phelps sank back in his chair. 'My head whirls[5],' said he; 'your words have dazed me[6].'

'The principal difficulty in your case,' remarked Holmes, in his didactic fashion, 'lay in the fact of there being too much evidence[7]. What was vital was overlaid[8] and hidden by what was irrelevant[9]. Of all the facts which were presented to us, we had to pick just those which we deemed to be[10] essential, and then piece them together in their order[11], so as to reconstruct this very remarkable chain of events. I had already begun to suspect Joseph, from the fact that you had intended to travel home with him that night, and that therefore[12] it was a likely enough thing[13] that he should call for you[14] – knowing the Foreign Office well – upon his way. When I heard that someone had been so anxious to[15] get into the bedroom, in which no one but[16] Joseph could have concealed[17] anything – you told us in your narrative[18] how you had turned Joseph out[19] when you arrived with the doctor – my suspicions all changed to certainties, especially as the attempt was made on the first night upon which the nurse was absent, showing that the intruder was well acquainted with the[20] ways[21] of the house.'

'How blind[22] I have been!'

'The facts of the case, as far as I have worked them out[23], are these: This Joseph Harrison

1. en boursicotant
2. se renflouer
3. égoïste
4. le retenir
5. tourne
6. m'ont abasourdi
7. venait de ce qu'il y avait trop d'indices
8. recouvert
9. hors de propos
10. considérions comme
11. les remettre dans l'ordre
12. donc
13. tout à fait plausible
14. vous rende visite
15. voulu à tout prix
16. hormis
17. dissimulé
18. récit
19. fait sortir Joseph
20. très au fait des
21. habitudes
22. Quel aveugle
23. tels que j'ai pu les reconstituer

entered the office through the Charles Street door, and knowing his way he walked straight into your room the instant after you left it. Finding no one there he promptly[1] rang the bell, and at the instant that he did so his eyes caught the paper upon the table. A glance[2] showed him that chance had put in his way a State document of immense value, and in a flash he had thrust it into his pocket and was gone. A few minutes elapsed[3], as you remember, before the sleepy commissionaire drew your attention to the bell, and those were just enough to give the thief time to make his escape[4].

'He made his way to Woking by the first train, and, having examined his booty[5], and assured himself that it really was of immense value, he concealed it in what he thought was a very safe place, with the intention of taking it out again in a day or two, and carrying it to the French Embassy, or wherever he thought that a long price was to be had[6]. Then came your sudden return. He, without a moment's warning[7], was bundled out[8] of his room, and from that time onwards[9] there were always at least two of you there to prevent him from regaining his treasure. The situation to him must have been a maddening one[10]. But at last he thought he saw his chance[11]. He tried to steal in[12], but was baffled[13] by your wakefulness[14]. You may remember that you did not take your usual draught[15] that night.'

'I remember.'

'I fancy that he had taken steps to make that draught efficacious, and that he quite relied upon your being[16] unconscious. Of course, I understood that he would repeat the attempt[17] whenever it could be done with safety. Your leaving the room gave him the chance he wanted. I kept Miss Harrison in it all day, so that he might not anticipate us[18].

1. aussitôt
2. simple regard
3. se sont écoulées
4. de prendre la fuite
5. butin
6. qu'il pourrait en obtenir une somme substantielle
7. sans préavis
8. délogé
9. dès lors,
10. exaspérante
11. l'occasion a semblé se présenter
12. de s'introduire discrètement
13. pris de court
14. le fait que vous ne dormiez pas
15. sirop [somnifère]
16. comptait bien que vous seriez
17. tentative
18. ne nous devance pas

1. la voie était libre

2. d'arracher

3. les plinthes

4. me suis ainsi épargné

5. alors qu'il

6. devait seulement servir d'outil

7. à la compassion duquel

8. je répugnerais fort

9. à compter

Then, having given him the idea that the coast was clear[1], I kept guard as I have described. I already knew that the papers were probably in the room, but I had no desire to rip up[2] all the planking and skirting[3] in search of them. I let him take them, therefore, from the hiding-place, and so saved myself[4] an infinity of trouble. Is there any other point which I can make clear?'

'Why did he try the window on the first occasion,' I asked, 'when he[5] might have entered by the door?'

'In reaching the door he would have to pass seven bedrooms. On the other hand, he could get out on to the lawn with ease. Anything else?'

'You do not think,' asked Phelps, 'that he had any murderous intention? The knife was only meant as a tool[6].'

'It may be so,' answered Holmes, shrugging his shoulders. 'I can only say for certain that Mr. Joseph Harrison is a gentleman to whose mercy[7] I should be extremely unwilling[8] to trust[9].'

La collection Yes you can!

Les faux débutants

Linwood Barclay *Broken Promise*

M. C. Beaton *Agatha Raisin and the Quiche of Death* ✦ *Agatha Raisin and the Vicious Vet* ✦ *Agatha Raisin and the Potted Gardener* ✦ *Death of a Gossip*

Harlan Coben *The Stranger*

Michael Connelly *The Black Box* ✦ *The Burning Room* ✦ *The Drop* ✦ *The Wrong Side of Goodbye*

Ken Follett *The Modigliani Scandal*

Mary Higgins Clark *A Cry in the Night*
A Stranger is Watching
Loves Music, Loves to Dance
Where are the Children?

Anthony Horowitz *The House of Silk*

George R. R. Martin *The Hedge Knight* ✦ *The Sworn Sword* ✦ *The Mystery Knight*

Ian Rankin *In a House of Lies* ✦ *Knots & Crosses*

Nicholas Sparks *Message in a Bottle*

Les intermédiaires

Harlan Coben *Caught* ✦ *Play Dead* ✦ *Stay Close* ✦ *Tell No One* ✦ *The Woods*

Ken Follett *Paper Money*

Anthony Horowitz *Moriarty*

P. D. James *A Mind to Murder* ✦ *Death Comes to Pemberley*

Douglas Kennedy *The Big Picture*

Stephen King *Finders Keepers* ✦ *The Green Mile*

John le Carré *A Most Wanted Man*

Les avancés

Paul Auster	*Leviathan* ✦ *Oracle Night* ✦
Julian Barnes	*The Sense of an Ending*
Michael Cunningham	*By Nightfall* ✦ *The Hours*
Helen Fielding	*Bridget Jones's Diary* ✦ *Bridget Jones: The Edge of Reason*
Elizabeth George	*A Great Deliverance*
Stephen King	*Dolores Claiborne* ✦ *Misery*

Les classiques

Jane Austen	*Northanger Abbey* ✦ *Pride and Prejudice*
Charlotte Brontë	*Jane Eyre*
G. K. Chesterton	*The Innocence of Father Brown*
Arthur Conan Doyle	*A Study in Scarlet* ✦ *Five Adventures of Sherlock Holmes* ✦ *The Hound of the Baskervilles*
Francis Scott Fitzgerald	*Tender is the Night* ✦ *The Great Gatsby*
Washington Irving, A. Conan Doyle, Edgar Allan Poe	*The Legend of Sleepy Hollow* *and Other Scary Stories*
H. P. Lovecraft	*The Call of Cthulhu and Other Weird Stories*
George Orwell	*Animal Farm* ✦ *1984*
Edgar Allan Poe	*The Fall of the House of Usher* *and Other Scary Stories*
Mary Shelley	*Frankenstein*
Bram Stoker	*Dracula*
Edith Wharton	*The Age of Innocence*
Oscar Wilde	*The Importance of Being Earnest* ✦ *The Picture of Dorian Gray*
Virginia Woolf	*To the Lighthouse*

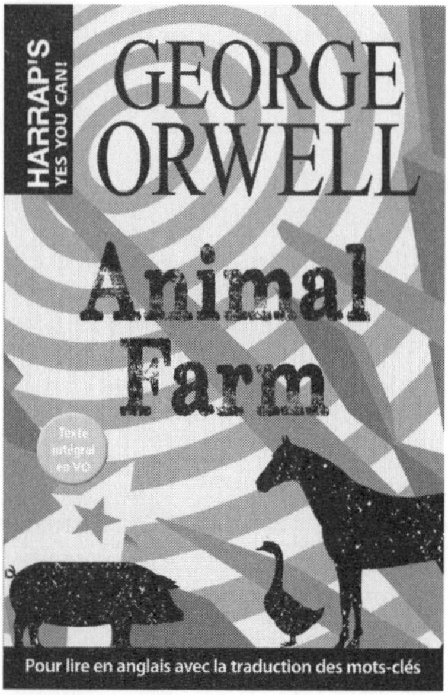

PAPIER À BASE DE FIBRES CERTIFIÉES

HARRAP s'engage pour l'environnement en réduisant l'empreinte carbone de ses livres. Celle de cet exemplaire est de : 600 g éq. CO_2 Rendez-vous sur www.larousse-durable.fr

Imprimé en Italie par Grafica Veneta
Dépôt légal : mai 2022
330863-03/ 11055972 – mars 2024